I0749186

Pecos Reckoning

A Fernando Lopez Santa Fe Mystery

Pecos Reckoning

A Fernando Lopez Santa Fe Mystery

James C. Wilson

Santa Fe

Sunstone books may be purchased for educational, business, or sales promotional use.
For information please write: Special Markets Department, Sunstone Press,
P.O. Box 2321, Santa Fe, New Mexico 87504-2321.
Printed on acid-free paper

Library of Congress Cataloging-in-Publication Data

Names: Wilson, James C., 1948- author. | Sunstone Press, publisher. | Wilson, James C., 1948- Fernando Lopez Santa Fe mystery.
Title: Pecos reckoning : a Fernando Lopez Santa Fe mystery / James C. Wilson.
Description: Santa Fe : Sunstone Press, [2023] | Series: A Fernando Lopez Santa Fe mystery | Contains readers guide. | Summary: "When the infamous Foreman of Three Hills Ranch reappears in Santa Fe looking to take revenge for his conviction for sex trafficking at the notorious ranch, Private Inspector Fernando Lopez finds himself a hunted man, lured to the Pecos Wilderness and into the Foreman's trap"-- Provided by publisher.
Identifiers: LCCN 2023057006 | ISBN 9781632936530 (paperback) | ISBN 9781611397383 (epub)
Subjects: LCSH: Lopez, Fernando (Fictitious character) | Murder--Investigation--Fiction. | Human trafficking--New Mexico--Santa Fe--Fiction. | LCGFT: Detective and mystery fiction.
Classification: LCC PS3623.I58485 P43 2023 | DDC 813.6--dc23/eng/20240117
LC record available at https://lccn.loc.gov/2023057006

WWW.SUNSTONEPRESS.COM
SUNSTONE PRESS / POST OFFICE BOX 2321 / SANTA FE, NM 87504-2321 /USA
(505) 988-4418

Before you embark on a journey of revenge, dig two graves.
—Confucius

Ambush

Santa Fe Police Sargent Matt Medina had just left the scene of an armed robbery. Two young punks had robbed and pistol-whipped an elderly clerk at a Seven Eleven on Cerrillos Road earlier this evening. The dumbasses came away with less than twenty dollars, having forgotten that almost everyone pays with credit cards these days, not cash. The clerk refused a ride to the Emergency Room after a couple of EMTs cleaned him up. The clerk had only the vaguest description of the two punks. To make matters worse, the store's security cameras weren't working. How the hell was he supposed to track down the perpetrators without a description or a video image? No, it would be yet another crime without consequences for the perpetrators, unsolved and soon forgotten. But one of these days the punks would encounter a clerk with a gun and get their just rewards. The sooner, the better. That's what he told the clerk.

The call came just as he climbed into his cruiser and pulled out onto Cerrillos Road. He recognized the voice of Don, the evening dispatcher at the Washington Avenue Station: active shooter at the homeless camp in Fort Marcy Park, several shots fired, one down. Matt hadn't been to the homeless camp since Old Bill died a year ago, beaten to death by a group of vigilantes who wanted to rid Santa Fe of its growing homeless and immigrant communities. To his knowledge, there hadn't been any trouble at the camp since.

Matt turned off the radio and hit the siren. He drove fast down Cerrillos Road and around Paseo de Peralta to Bishop's Lodge Road. He screamed through the turn and shot down Bishop's Lodge Road to Morales, where he turned left and entered the dimly lit Fort Marcy Park. Thick clouds blotted out the moon, plunging the park into darkness. The only light came from intermittent streetlights along the road. Spaced far apart, the lamps cast feeble circles of yellow light as he drove by toward the homeless camp at the back of the park. When he saw the campfires straight ahead, near Arroyo Barranca, he turned into the parking lot and coasted to a dark corner of the lot. Then he climbed out of his cruiser as silently as possible.

He paused a moment to let his eyes adjust to the darkness, listening for any sound of danger. He heard muffled voices coming from the camp, but no one shouting or arguing. No sign of an active shooter, which puzzled him. An active shooter generates bedlam and hysteria, not chit chat over a campfire. Especially when one person is already down.

Before moving away from his cruiser, Matt reached for his service pistol but then had second thoughts. Better to check out the situation first; he didn't want to provoke a confrontation with the shooter, if he did exist. So he eased out into the dark night, walking slowly toward the camp. He could make out shapes of trees in the darkness, shadows deepening into shadows. Otherwise, no one appeared and nothing stirred, only muffled voices coming out of the darkness, like disembodied spirits. Or like ghosts returning to look for whatever they'd left behind.

He followed a well-worn path, stepping gingerly so as to make as little noise as possible. The campfires ahead grew larger as he came closer. The acrid smoke stung his nostrils. If he didn't know better, he would think the arroyo was on fire.

Suddenly he heard a twig snap off to his right. He froze, his hand once again moving down to his holster. The cold, hard metal of his Glock 19 comforted him. He started to lift his gun but stopped when he saw the culprit: an emaciated dog loping through the trees. Looked sickly, a stray probably. Turning back to the path, he continued on into the night.

Just ahead a hulking shadow materialized in the darkness, silhouetted against the campfires. Matt saw a large man with huge shoulders walking out of the smoke toward him. The shooter?

Matt stopped, unsure of what to do. His hand touched his holster, ready.

Then the man in the shadows stopped, as if to take a look at Matt. "Not the one I want, but you'll do," the man said in a deep gravelly voice.

"What do you–" Matt began as the man's arm came up holding a pistol that fired once, twice.

The first bullet struck Matt in the chest and buckled him. The second bullet sliced through his brain as he fell.

1

Private Investigator Fernando Lopez sat in his office on Canyon Road brooding. He hadn't had a client in over a week now. Not one. In fact, he'd had only two clients in the month since he'd returned from Taos helping Taos County Sheriff Hank Mathews with the dead woman at the Sagebrush Inn and the feud between the Ryan and Lucero Clans, which turned out to be the same damn case. He hated to be idle. After thirty years as a detective in the Santa Fe Police Department, Fernando needed to keep busy. When he had too much time to brood, too many bad memories perked up from his murky unconscious, too much guilt and too many regrets. Better to stay busy and not revisit the past.

Problem was, Fernando didn't have any business at the moment. About the only productive thing he'd been doing was helping his friend and landlord Ruby Montez take care of Wayne Fontenot, an old painter who lived on Upper Canyon Road. Nearing 90, Wayne had a myriad of physical problems, including A-fib, high blood pressure, and now full-blown Alzheimer's. Wayne had no family and very few friends, since he tended to be quarrelsome and more likely than not intoxicated. So Ruby checked on Wayne daily, bringing him both breakfast and dinner. Fernando subbed for Ruby whenever she had a conflict.

Fernando drove down to his office every morning, usually between nine and ten o'clock. His office had been the garage of an old carriage house that Ruby let him use rent-free. He'd added wood paneling, carpeting, and office furniture. Since retiring, he took his sweet time in the morning. All day, really. If he wasn't working, he usually called it quits around four o'clock and headed either home to his sweet adobe on Acequia Madre Street or down Canyon Road to the El Farol bar for drinks. The artists on Canyon Road gathered religiously at El Farol every afternoon for happy hour and to bitch about the tourists. None of them bitched louder than his landlord Ruby, a potter who owned a gallery next door in the remodeled carriage house and a pottery co-op down in the Railyard District.

A few minutes before four o'clock, Fernando said the hell with it. He decided to stop at El Farol for a quick Modelo and then go home to work in the garden with his wife, Estelle. Before leaving, he made sure his filing cabinet was locked. Then he grabbed his cell phone and changed his window sign from 'Open' to 'Closed.' When he opened the door to leave, he was surprised to see Manny Alvarez walking down the path to his office. Manny, Fernando's replacement as lead detective at the Santa Fe Police Department, had just returned to active duty. He'd taken a three-month medical leave after receiving serious injuries in a shootout with gang members of the Sinaloa Cartel on Upper Canyon Road. Since then the Sinaloa presence in Santa Fe had grown quietly, under the radar, so to speak. Both sides looked the other way in order to preserve a fragile peace. Don't ask, don't tell.

"Hey, Fernando," Manny said quietly. Since the shootout, Manny had been rather subdued. A small man in his early forties with prematurely thinning hair, Manny looked frail today, low on energy. He seemed to have lost weight, which showed on his thin face with hollowed out cheeks.

"Damn, you look serious, amigo," Fernando said. "Who died?"

'Matt Medina," Manny replied.

Fernando stopped laughing. "I was joking. What happened to Matt?"

Manny motioned toward Fernando's office. "Can we talk?"

"Sure, come on in," Fernando said, holding the door open for Manny, who took a seat across from his desk.

Fernando sat at the desk waiting.

"Okay, here's the scoop, it looks like we have a serial cop killer on the loose in Santa Fe," Manny said, sighing. "Matt was set up and ambushed last night in Fort Marcy Park, near the homeless camp. Someone called in a report of a shooter with one person down about nine o'clock. When Matt arrived he ran into an ambush. He was shot twice, both of them fatal. He died instantly, never had a chance."

"Christ!" Fernando said, remembering Matt as a likable fellow and a conscientious cop.

"Thing is, one of the people at the homeless camp heard the shooter say, 'Not the one I want, but you'll do,' right before he shot Matt," Manny said, shaking his head. "In other words, the shooter was looking for another cop, not Matt. We have no idea who he was after."

Fernando nodded. "Okay, but why do you think this is a serial killer?"

"Because Sean Beatty was set up and ambushed the same way last week on Siler Road," Manny said. "Exactly the same M.O., with the same

Glock nine millimeter weapon. The guy's looking for someone, some cop he holds a grudge against, but in the meantime, he'll shoot any cop he encounters. We may need to identify him in order to find out who he's looking for."

"You think it's the Sinaloa Cartel again?" Fernando asked.

Manny shook his head. "No, we don't think so. It's not the way they operate. And Silva–you remember Silva Archivada, the head of Sinaloa in New Mexico? He seems to be trying to run a legit business out in Pojoaque."

"I remember," Fernando said. "He bought the old Line Camp honkytonk and remodeled it."

Manny nodded. "It's back in business again as a saloon/dancehall."

Fernando laughed. "With a little side business in the back room."

"I'm sure, but fortunately Line Camp is in Pojoaque, which is out of our jurisdiction," Manny said, pausing. "Anyway, I just wanted to let you know about the shooter, so you could be on guard. You were in the department for thirty years, so I'm sure you've made your share of enemies. Until we know who the shooter's hunting for, I'd watch my step."

Fernando didn't know what to say, so he simply said, "Thanks."

Manny smiled. "Come to think of it, you have lots of enemies, probably more than the rest of us."

"So Ruby and everyone else keeps telling me. I didn't know I was that popular," Fernando said, pleased that Manny's sense of humor was coming back.

Manny laughed.

"So how are you feeling?" Fernando asked. "Have you recovered from the surgeries? You still look a little frail."

"Pretty much," Manny said, sighing. "I lost a kidney and part of my large intestine...and I still feel, I don't know....just not quite up to speed. I've lost a step. I don't know how else to explain it."

"Understandable," Fernando said.

"But the worst part is that I've become a little gun shy," Manny said. "I'm tired of dealing with all these thugs who carry around assault weapons. I thought about retiring, but at my age I would have to find another job, and what else could I do? This job is the only thing I've ever been good at."

"Hell, you could join me as a private investigator," Fernando said.

Manny looked around. "Yeah, but do you have any business?"

"Not much, but the perks are good. You get to spend your days on Canyon Road and drink at El Farol every afternoon."

Manny laughed and stood up to leave.

Fernando watched as Manny walked out of his office and closed the door behind him.

Alone, Fernando reflected on Manny's news. He had, indeed, made a lot of enemies over the last thirty years. Probably more than anyone else at the station, with the possible exception of Sargent Antonio Blake, who had accompanied Fernando on most of his cases over the past ten years or so. Now Fernando worried the shooter might want to kill one or both of them as payback for whatever they'd done to him. Revenge could be a powerful drug, driving a man to do terrible things—and to take chances he wouldn't otherwise take.

Fernando sat at his desk brooding. Finally a way forward occurred to him. He took a yellow legal pad out of his desk and made a list of his recent cases and the names of the criminals they'd apprehended who might want revenge. Problem was, almost all of them were either dead or in jail. Of the ones who survived and weren't in jail, none of them stood out any more than the others. Each was as likely as the next to want to even the score. Cursing, he wadded up the paper and tossed it into his trash. This was a waste of time. If the shooter wanted to settle an old score with him, then Fernando would deal with that when the time came. Antonio, too, was more than capable of taking care of himself.

Finished, he locked up and walked down the gravel path to the parking lot. He decided to forego El Farol this afternoon since it was getting late. Instead, he climbed into his Cherokee and drove down to the Paseo and around to Acequia Madre Street. Moments later he pulled into the driveway leading to their cozy little adobe that dated from the 1920s. It set back from the street, among a row of huge, walled houses that had been remodeled into million-dollar mansions by wealthy newcomers from the East and West Coasts. The rich newcomers had driven up housing prices so much that old Santa Fe families could no longer afford to live in Santa Fe. Just this year the median price of a house in Santa Fe topped $700.000. He and Estelle had paid a whopping $50,000 for their little adobe forty years ago, before Santa Fe turned into Disneyland Southwest.

Fernando parked in the driveway and walked though their garden, under towering cottonwood trees. When he opened the back door, he found Estelle in the kitchen placing a tray of enchiladas in the oven, leftovers from last night's meal at La Choza. Fernando smiled when he saw how youthful she looked in jeans and a cotton sweater. Petite and athletic, Estelle hadn't lost her energy or her looks. Her black hair was only beginning to streak with gray, while his was all salt and no pepper. Unlike his deeply lined face, Estelle's was virtually free of wrinkles. No doubt about it, she had aged much better than he had.

"Leftovers tonight," Estelle said as he walked into the kitchen.

"Sound's good," Fernando said. He quickly set their kitchen table and then went to the refrigerator and grabbed a Modelo.

Over dinner Fernando told her about Manny's visit. "They think the shooter's after one particular cop, but they don't know who."

"Oh great, you're worried about a cop killer, and you're not even a cop anymore," Estelle said. "What aren't you telling me?"

"Yeah, but I busted a lot of criminals in my thirty years at the department," Fernando said. "They just want me to watch my step. I've been racking my brains trying to think of likely suspects, but I can't think of anyone in particular. I suppose everyone I busted would like to get back at me."

Estelle turned and stared at him. "Well, you just better be careful. You're supposed to be retired now, remember?"

Fernando nodded and opened his Modelo. "Don't worry. I'll be careful."

Estelle rolled her eyes.

2

Someone was shaking him awake. Fernando opened his eyes and saw Estelle standing over him framed by a slash of morning light coming through their bedroom window. Already dressed, she looked about to leave for work at her immigrant outreach program. She was saying something about a phone call that he didn't quite catch. He took a deep breath and tried to clear his head.

"Did you hear me?" she asked. "You have a phone call on the land line in the kitchen. I think it's your girlfriend."

Fernando knew she meant Ruby, who called often about Wayne Fontenot, now that the two of them were checking on Wayne daily. Estelle didn't like Ruby. Lots of people didn't like Ruby.

He and Ruby went back a long way, even before he met and married Estelle. Always prickly, Ruby wore her bad attitude with pride. To her, it was a badge of honor. Her in-your-face personality put off many people but had made her a force in Santa Fe politics for over two decades. A potter by trade, Ruby had risen through the ranks of *La Raza* to become the most progressive member of City Council ever. Back in the 1990s she fought tooth and nail against all the greedy developers who wanted to turn downtown Santa Fe into one big shopping mall. She led rallies, marches, protests, sit-ins, and if you believed the rumors, a fire-bombing or two.

She lost, of course. The developers and the Sotheby's crowd turned Santa Fe into Disneyland Southwest. The tide of gentrification sweeping over Santa Fe during those years hollowed out the city. Gone were most of the people whose families had lived in Santa Fe for generations. Increasingly higher home values and property taxes priced out all who couldn't afford the million-dollar homes. After two tumultuous terms on City Council lecturing, berating, cajoling, and threatening the other members, she said 'fuck it' and retired to the pottery co-op she owned and ran with a number of other potters, most of them women.

Still she refused to be silenced. She made it a point to attend most Council meetings and give the members a piece of her mind. Every one of them feared Ruby's tirades. Occasionally her anger would get the better of her language and she would be asked to leave. Once a few years back City Council banned her for a year, but her lawyer, Raoul Garcia, sued their asses and got her reinstated in her front row seat staring down the Council.

Over the years he and Ruby had always been friendly, probably because they felt the same way about gentrification and Santa Fe politics in general. That is, they usually ended up on the losing side. So it goes.

Wondering what Ruby wanted now, Fernando climbed out of bed and shuffled into the kitchen. Estelle waved goodbye from the kitchen door as he picked up the phone. Off to work.

"Hey, Fernando," Ruby said. "Can you bring Wayne his breakfast this morning? I got a situation down at the co-op. One of our kilns blew a circuit and caused a minor fire. An electrician is coming to fix it first thing this morning, if the bastard shows up. You know how that goes."

"Uh...sure, no problem," Fernando said. "How's Wayne doing? I haven't been over there for a couple of days."

"Not good," Ruby admitted. "In some ways he's still the cranky old fart that we know and love, but his mind wanders. One minute he'll be in the here and now, the next he'll be back at Claude's in the 1970s, so it's damned near impossible to follow his train of thought. Plus he's losing his fine motor ability. He can't do the little things with his hands, like using a knife and fork to eat. I try to bring him finger foods now, like a young kid."

"Okay, I'll pick him up a breakfast burrito," Fernando said. "He should be able to handle that."

"Good. Ask him if he wants to go to El Farol for our usual happy hour gathering," Ruby said. "I could pick him up on my way."

"I'll let you know," Fernando said and clicked off.

Still groggy, Fernando jumped in the shower and let the warm water wash over him for a few minutes, which was longer than he usually stayed in the shower. Then he shaved, dressed, and headed to the kitchen for a quick breakfast of leftovers, whatever he could find in the refrigerator. He was too lazy to make himself a hot breakfast this morning.

After finishing his second cup of coffee, Fernando locked up and climbed into his Cherokee. He drove around the Paseo to Cerrillos Road, clogged by fast food restaurants and cheap motels. It was just the place to find a quick breakfast burrito. He stopped at the first fast food joint he saw and bought a burrito, juice and coffee. Then he drove back around the Paseo to Canyon Road. When he entered Upper Canyon Road he looked for the familiar alley that would take him to Wayne's house. He always remembered the alley by the bright blue adobe house on one corner. When he spotted it he turned into the alley and drove up a slight hill to Wayne's yard, which was littered with cast-off furniture and piles of trash. So much so that it looked like a garbage dump rather than a yard. No sign of Wayne outside, although the front door of his tumbledown adobe remained wide open.

Fernando parked and set the brake. Every time he came here Wayne's adobe looked shabbier. Today he noticed more patches of cracked and fallen stucco, revealing the brown adobe bricks underneath. The roof sagged in the middle, threatening to collapse altogether. The dark windows looked as though they hadn't been washed in decades. A ghost house, soon to become one for real.

"Wayne?" Fernando called as he stepped through the open doorway.

No answer.

Wayne sat in one of his two stuffed chairs in the cluttered living area, his head drooping to his chest. He no longer wore his decades-old black suit. His visiting nurse who came to check on him once a day had provided him with gray sweatpants and a long-sleeve T-shirt. He wore slip-on sandals instead of his usual leather shoes.

Fernando grabbed Wayne's shoulder and shook the old man gently.

Wayne looked up at Fernando. "What?"

"Brought you some food," Fernando said. "One of your favorites, a breakfast burrito with sausage and egg and green chile."

"Okay," Wayne said, his version of thank you, two words Fernando had never heard him say.

Fernando found a plate in the kitchen cabinet and brought it to the table, where he unpacked the food and placed it on the plate. He took the lids off the coffee and juice containers. Then he helped Wayne over to the table and sat down across from the old man. Wayne sat staring at the plate for a long minute as if he were trying to levitate the burrito off the plate and into his mouth. No luck. The burrito stubbornly remained on the plate, inert.

"Go on, eat," Fernando said again.

With his hands shaking, Wayne picked up the burrito and took a small bite followed by a drink of coffee. While he nibbled at the food Fernando looked around the messy, two-room adobe. Wayne's easels and painting supplies took up most of the room, with a scattering of finished paintings stacked on the floor and leaning against the rear wall. The stack hadn't changed in years since Wayne no longer painted. Surveying the mess, Fernando thought the sensible thing would be to clear out the whole damn two rooms and demolish the decrepit house, but that would have to wait until Wayne was gone. Wayne refused to leave his house. And he refused to let anyone touch his paintings or clean up the area around his easels.

Wayne drank the coffee and juice but only managed to eat about half the burrito before he tired and had to be helped back to his stuffed chair. The old man immediately fell asleep. Fernando sat across from Wayne in the second stuffed chair and watched him sleep. Not much he could do. Wayne didn't seem interested in much of anything anymore. Just waiting for the end, it seemed. That thought depressed Fernando, who had his own troubles staying away from the dark place.

Before leaving, Fernando put the uneaten food in the refrigerator with all the other half-eaten meals and cleaned up the mess Wayne had made on and around the table. Then Fernando left, closing the door behind him quietly so as not to wake Wayne. Glad to be out of there.

Once outside, he took a deep breath of fresh air and shook his head, trying to shake off the dark place that waited just below the surface of his consciousness, threatening to surface.

The proverbial beast in the jungle.

3

The early morning sun bathed Canyon Road in a glorious blue light as Fernando drove down to his office. The first tourists of the day began appearing on Canyon Road, some out for their morning strolls and others window shopping, waiting for the galleries to open. The slant of light and the cool Alpine air meant they had reached the cusp of Fall. Before he knew it the fragrant smell of piñon smoke would be in the air. The morning freshness cheered Fernando as he turned into his parking lot between Ruby's gallery on one side and Essentia, the sex shop, on the other.

Fernando parked his Cherokee behind Ruby's Honda Accord and climbed out, thinking he might stop in and visit Ruby later this morning. Maybe the two of them could have lunch at El Farol. He walked around to the front of the Cherokee and admired his hand-carved wooden sign at the head of the path leading to his office. The sign read 'Fernando Lopez, Private Investigator,' under a cut-out of an eye–meaning, of course, a private eye. He heard a car slowing down on Canyon Road just as he stepped on the gravel path. A possible client coming to see him? That would be a welcome change. He turned to look, expecting to see the car pulling into his parking lot.

Suddenly a gunshot shattered the perfect morning: Pop!

Fernando dove headfirst onto the gravel, scraping his hands on the loose gravel. He heard the bullet shatter one of the Cherokee's windows.

Three more shots followed: Pop! Pop! Pop! Two of the bullets smashed into his sign. The third bullet kicked up sand at the top of the gravel path.

Fernando clawed his way to his feet and drew his Smith & Wesson, crouching behind the cab of the Cherokee. He saw the car, a white sedan, as it tore off down Canyon Road. Looked like only one person inside, the driver.

Fernando took aim but held his fire because of a group tourists walking on Canyon Road. Too dangerous. He could kill someone if he fired.

Fernando took a deep breath. Good thing the gunman had shot from a moving vehicle and not a fixed position. Otherwise he would be a dead man.

Starting to calm down, he inspected the driver's side window on his Cherokee, which the first bullet had shattered. Moments later Ruby stuck her head out of her gallery and yelled, "What happened? Is someone hurt?"

"Everyone's okay," Fernando yelled back.

Ruby walked cautiously off her porch into the parking lot. "Fernando? What the fuck?"

Fernando smiled at the sight of Ruby. Her shoulder length black hair might be streaked with gray, but she was still the striking woman Fernando knew from his youth: black, bedroom eyes and an irreverent smile that radiated sexuality. She wore tight jeans and a black silk blouse unbuttoned to the center of her chest. She looked like a million bucks.

Moments later Paul and June Bryan, the owners of Essentia, came creeping out of their sex shop one cautious step at a time. They relaxed when they saw Fernando and Ruby, walking over to join them. All four of them stared at his sign. Two of the bullets fired by the gunman had hit the sign, one in the eye and the other in Fernando's last name. Lopez now read Lope.

Ruby seemed to think the bullet holes were funny. "Hmmm, I wonder if your customers will think the bullet holes are badges of honor? You know, bring in more troubled people looking for a hired gun."

Paul, on the other hand, was dead serious. "No, this is bad. Bad for all of our businesses. Customers will stay away."

"I'm joking, you idiot," Ruby said. Ruby was a force of nature, gorgeous but intimidating.

"I just meant–" Paul started to say but stopped, a clean-cut, yuppified young man wearing his usual chinos and navy polo. He looked as though he'd just wandered in off a golf course.

"We just think the sign needs to be replaced soon or we'll all lose business," June explained, a tiny young woman with blue hair wearing a skimpy yoga leotard that made her look half naked. June was a licensed masseuse and yoga instructor, both of which she practiced in one of the therapy rooms at Essentia.

Fernando nodded, hands on hips. Every time he'd seen June, she'd been wearing a leotard. He wondered if she ever took them off. To sleep?

The four of them stared at the sign.

"Well, shit," Fernando said finally. "I'll have to get Bennie Ortiz over here to see if he can repair it. I'd ask him to make another sign, but If I do, whoever did this will probably just shoot up the sign again."

"Waste of money," Ruby said. She stepped up to the sign and poked her fingers through the bullet holes in the wood. "Yeah, Bennie can probably put a couple of wood plugs in the holes. Little paint and it'll look as good as new."

Fernando ran his fingers over the sign. "You think?"

Paul and June lost interest and wandered back to Essentia, leaving Fernando and Ruby to continue their conversation.

"Do you have any idea who did this?" Ruby asked.

Fernando shrugged. "Yeah. I mean no, not exactly. It's a long story."

"Come into the gallery and tell me about it," Ruby said, turning away.

Fernando followed her to the porch of her gallery, which she'd named Three Cities of Spain after a historic restaurant on Canyon Road that had closed decades ago. Inside, the gallery's walls and shelves were a riot of color: vibrant acrylic and oil paintings hung on the walls, while colorful ceramics filled the shelves that Ruby added to accommodate the pottery produced in her pottery co-op down in the Railyard District. Previously the gallery had been her ex-husband Jimmy Mackey's painting studio before he was murdered in Taos.

Fernando joined Ruby in her office. They sat at a make-shift counter Ruby used for lunches and coffee breaks. "Is it too early for a beer?" Ruby asked.

Fernando checked his watch. Half past eleven o'clock. "Probably."

"I'll take that as a no," Ruby said. She pulled two beers out of a mini fridge under the counter and opened them. "You want a glass?"

Fernando shook his head. Ruby and the other artists on Canyon Road who hung out at El Farol were known to be serious drinkers. Each and every one of them could drink him under the table.

"So what's the scoop?" Ruby asked. Do you, or do you not know the asshole who shot up your sign?"

"Not exactly," Fernando said. He told Ruby about the cop killer in town who so far had killed two officers, Matt Medina and Sean Beatty.

"At random?" Ruby asked. "Is he killing cops at random, whoever he happens to encounter?"

Fernando shook his head. "Manny thinks he's after someone in particular, someone who arrested him or whatever. To get revenge."

Ruby stared at him.

Fernando stared back.

"Jesus, Fernando," Ruby said. "What are you saying, that the shooter might be after you?"

Fernando shrugged. "I don't know what to think. Maybe."

"Do you have any idea who it could be?" Ruby asked. "Someone who wants to get back at you?"

"Hah! They would have to line up," Fernando said. "Off-hand I can think of dozens of people who might want revenge. I busted a lot of people in the thirty years I was in the department."

Ruby nodded. "So what are you going to do?"

Fernando threw up his hands. "I have no idea. I can't just hide out all day in my office. Life goes on."

"Or doesn't," Ruby said. "Remember, you got a lot of enemies."

"So you keep saying," Fernando replied, finishing his beer.

"You know what, I have Jimmy's old pistol around here somewhere," Ruby said, looking around her office. "I can probably find it. You want me to get it out so I can give you a hand in case this asshole comes back? I used to be a pretty good shot back in the day."

Fernando smiled. "I remember the night you threatened to bring a gun to the City Council meeting."

"Hah! They're lucky I didn't," Ruby shot back.

"And every one of those losers knew it," Fernando said.

"Yeah, that was the group responsible for the Disneyfication of the Plaza," Ruby said. "They should have been shot for what they did to the Plaza. No, all I'm saying is that I can help out if you need me. I can back you up."

"Thanks, but I'll take care of it," Fernando said, standing up from the counter. He waved and walked out of the gallery and back to his office. Once inside he closed and locked the door behind him, suddenly feeling paranoid.

Sitting at his desk, he took his Smith & Wesson out of its holster and placed it on his desktop. He felt uneasy, at loose ends after the morning ambush. He'd become the hunted, whereas in the past he'd always been the hunter. He didn't like the feeling of not knowing what was going to happen next. He hated waiting, anticipating. It drove him crazy. He needed to act.

With that Fernando walked over and unlocked his office door. If the sonofabitch wanted a piece of him, let him come. Whoever it was.

4

Estelle had already left for work by the time Fernando awoke. He had no idea what time she had returned last night, because he'd fallen asleep early and slept like the dead. Estelle insisted on keeping her job, which she loved. Unlike Fernando, who cut back his workload once he retired, Estelle worked long hours for the Saint Francis Immigrant Outreach Program, a church-sponsored nonprofit that provided food and clothing and other services to Santa Fe's growing immigrant community. In fact, her workload kept increasing as each year more and more immigrants came through Santa Fe, a sanctuary city. An ancient city of three cultures founded in 1610, most people in Santa Fe were damn proud of its designation as a sanctuary city.

Fernando hated to admit it, but he and Estelle were no longer as close as they once were. Estelle had grown more religious over the years, working for the outreach program and attending mass almost every Sunday. He had grown in the opposite direction, no longer finding his meaning in church doctrine. Estelle accepted the meaning prescribed by the Catholic Church, whereas he believed in a material world, where you created your own meaning by what you did, your actions. His friend and sometime arch enemy Raoul Garcia, the best (and certainly the most radical) criminal lawyer in the state of New Mexico and a would-be philosopher, said it best: "Fuck the dogma, the only thing that matters is what you do. Existence precedes essence, bro. Read some existentialism."

The belief that he had to create his own meaning drew him to law enforcement and later to private investigation, where he could do something that mattered, something that had value in and of itself and that went beyond the individual self to the community and contributed to the common good. He liked to think it was a profession that could—or should—make people's lives better. At any rate, it was a profession he could live with.

Fernando usually went to church with Estelle on Christmas Eve and

Easter Sunday because Estelle still found meaning in the church, but that was as far as he was willing to go.

Fernando splashed water on his face and dressed quickly, avoiding the mirror. He'd become superstitious about the mirror, believing every time he looked in the mirror he got older. If he stopped looking, he wouldn't age.

Dressed, Fernando went to the kitchen and poured himself a cup of cold coffee from the pot Estelle had left on the counter. He warmed it in the microwave and then made himself eggs and toast for breakfast.

Over breakfast Fernando decided to bring out the big hardware. He didn't want to take chances now that he knew, or at least suspected, that an unknown gunman had targeted him. So when he finished eating he went into his office and looked around. He'd forgotten where he stashed his sniper rifle. Eventually he found it high on a closet shelf, locked in its heavy gun case. He carried the case into the kitchen and placed it on the table. Good thing Estelle wasn't here. She hated the sniper rifle, and she would hate the sight of the gun case on her kitchen table.

Fernando unlocked the gun case and examined the Steyr SSG 69, an Austrian bolt-action rifle with scope. He hadn't used the rifle in at least ten years. So he sat at the kitchen table with his maintenance kit and cleaned and oiled the rifle using his spray scrubber and J-D Bore Cleaning Compound. Then he tightened the bolts on the scope and meticulously cleaned the lenses. He knew everything depended on the accuracy of the lenses.

Years ago he'd chosen the Steyr for two specific reasons: its lightness and its accuracy. The Steyr was deadeye up to seven or eight hundred meters. The literature said eight, but he had his doubts.

Fernando put the rifle back in its case just as his cell phone rang. He wasn't surprised when he saw the name on the phone; he'd been expecting Manny to call with an update.

"Manny, I have some news for you," Fernando said.

"Me too," Manny said. "You go first."

"Our shooter paid me a visit yesterday afternoon," Fernando said. "Surprised me when I was getting out of the Cherokee at my office parking lot. He missed me, but he busted out a side window in the Cherokee and put a couple of bullet holes in my private eye sign. I was fortunate he was shooting from a car speeding down Canyon Road. Otherwise I wouldn't be here talking to you now."

"No kidding! What did the car look like?" Manny asked.

"Some sort of white sedan," Fernando responded. "I didn't catch the make, it was going too fast. Looked like the driver was male."

"Yeah, that fits Antonio's description," Manny said.

Fernando paused. "What do you mean?"

"Antonio had a run-in with the shooter, too," Manny said. "He's in Christus Saint Vincent Hospital, room three-ten. I'm with him now."

Fernando cursed. "What happened?"

"I'll let Antonio tell you," Manny said. "They're talking about releasing him around Noon. He's arguing with the nurses right now."

Fernando laughed.

"He's one tough hombre," Manny added.

"Okay, I'm on my way," Fernando said. "I just need to make one stop at the auto glass shop on Cerrillos. To replace the front side window on the driver's side of the Cherokee."

"If I get called away, can you give Antonio a ride to his Jeep?" Manny asked. "I think it's back at the station."

"No problem," Fernando said.

After he clicked off, Fernando locked the house and carried his gun case to the Cherokee, placing it in the hidden compartment under the floorboards in the rear hatch. Then he drove to the Paseo and around to Cerrillos Road. His auto glass shop was about a mile down Cerrillos. Over the years he'd had so many windows shot out of his various vehicles that the shop owner laughed every time he showed up with another shattered window. But the benefit of having your windows shot out routinely was that the glass shop usually gave him fast service. They figured the sooner they got the Cherokee back on the street, the sooner some sonofabitch would shoot out another window for them to repair. Cha-ching!

Even so, because they were busy, it took them almost two hours to replace the window. By the time Fernando made it to Christus Saint Vincent it was nearly eleven o'clock.

Fernando parked near the front entrance, unsure of Antonio's condition. Manny hadn't given him any details. Inside the automatic doors he took an elevator up to the third floor. He heard Antonio's voice as soon as he stepped on the ward, not exactly angry but not exactly not angry either. Antonio was complaining about something to a nurse who was attempting to back out of his room. Fernando arrived just as the nurse fled down the hall to the nurse's station.

Fernando walked into the room and found Antonio sitting in a chair wearing his street clothes beside what had been his bed. He had a bulging bandage on his left arm under his shirt.

As soon as Antonio saw Fernando he stood up, all six foot, seven inches and two hundred and eighty pounds of him. "Just get me out of this fucking place," the big man said.

Fernando smiled. "Nice to see you too. What happened to you?"

Antonio frowned. "Long story. You wanna hear it now or later?"

"Now," Fernando said. "I just had an encounter with the shooter yesterday afternoon. Must be the same guy."

"You first," Antonio said.

Fernando recounted the drive-by shooting at his office.

"Could be the same guy, but my guy used a rifle," Antonio said. "He must have been waiting for me when I left the station at the end of my shift. I saw him in the rear view mirror on Old Santa Fe Trail. When we came to the Old Las Vegas Highway I slowed down to see if he would pass. He didn't. That's when I knew the motherfucker was trailing me."

"What color was his car?" Fernando interrupted.

"White. It was a white sedan, maybe an Impala. Kept following me down the highway at whatever speed I was going. Finally I got tired of the cat and mouse game, so I pulled into the Bobcat Bite driveway. You know, the old hamburger joint on the way to Apache Canyon."

Fernando nodded.

"There were only a couple of cars in the Bobcat Bite parking lot, so I drove behind the restaurant and parked my Jeep out of sight," Antonio said. "Then I walked around the corner of the building to take a look. That was my mistake. The shooter was standing in the driveway beside his car and aiming a rifle at me. I jumped to the side just as the rifle fired. The bullet nicked my upper arm as I fell. By the time I recovered enough to look around the corner again, he was driving away, probably because other cars were arriving. I put pressure on my wound, but it was bleeding like a sonofabitch, so I called nine one one. An ambulance picked me up and brought me here. I had to have my Jeep towed back to the station."

"Lucky you jumped," Fernando said.

"The docs told me the bullet grazed the bone in my upper arm," Antonio explained. "I'm waiting for my discharge papers now. I don't know what's taking them so damn long."

"It's not Noon yet," Fernando said.

"So what? I been sitting in that chair since eight o'clock."

Fernando had no response to that, so he took a seat on the other side of the bed. Antonio remained standing for a moment and then begrudgingly sat back down in his chair. They sat there in silence, staring at each other, until a nurse came into the room a few minutes before Noon with Antonio's walking papers. She stopped at the foot of the bed, keeping her distance from Antonio.

"Congratulations, Mr. Blake, I have discharge papers for you to sign," the nurse said, a young blond nurse with blue-rimmed glasses that matched her blue suit. "I know you're anxious to go." She looked at Fernando and rolled her eyes.

Fernando smiled.

"About time," Antonio said, reaching over and grabbing the clipboard. He signed the papers quickly and handed back the clipboard.

"Do you want me to get you a wheelchair?" the nurse asked.

Antonio scowled at the nurse and walked out of the room and down the hallway, Fernando following.

Once in the Cherokee Antonio unbuttoned his shirt and ripped off the bulky outer bandage on his arm and tossed it in the back of the vehicle. Fernando stared at him, not believing what he'd just witnessed.

"I have a high tolerance for pain," Antonio said. "Now take me to the station. I need to get to work."

5

After dropping off Antonio at the Washington Avenue Station, Fernando drove directly to his office on Canyon Road. He was debating whether to drive out to Bobcat Bite and ask if any of the employees had witnessed the shooting last night or had seen the white sedan parked along the highway, when he happened to notice the blinking light on his machine. Someone had left a message.

He hit the button and listened to a hoarse female voice: "Mister Lopez, I don't know if you remember me, but it's Ester Hoke. I live next door to Three Hills Ranch where that outfit of sex traffickers lived. They killed my husband, if you remember. The place has been vacant since you arrested them and killed that devil Warner who owned the place. But the last couple of nights there's been lights over there. I don't know if someone's camping there or if some homeless people moved in or what. I sure hope those sex traffickers don't come back. Anyway, I thought you should know. You told me to call anytime."

Fernando remembered Three Hills Ranch only too well. One of the most nightmarish cases in his years as a Santa Fe Police Detective. The case involved a wealthy scumbag from Los Angeles who set up a sex ranch for high-rollers. The scumbag, Robert Warner, kidnapped young women from border towns like Nogales and Juarez and brought them to the ranch to serve as sex slaves. Warner's thugs killed several of the young women who tried to escape. They also killed Ester Hoke's husband, A.J. Hoke, who reported the criminal activity. When the Santa Fe Police and County Sheriff finally busted the ranch, Warner died in a fiery helicopter crash attempting to flee the ranch. Several of Warner's men were arrested and sentenced to serious time in the big house. Not a pleasant memory. None of it.

Fernando dialed Ester Hoke's number and waited for her to answer. He was about to hang up when she answered.

"Mrs. Hoke, this is Fernando Lopez," Fernando said. "I got your message. I certainly do remember you and your husband. I'm so sorry we couldn't save him, he was a good man."

"Well…you did what you could," Ester said.

The woman sounded ancient. She must be in her mid-eighties by now, Fernando figured.

"You mentioned seeing lights over at Three Hill Ranch," Fernando said. "Have you seen any of the people who may be camping there? Anyone coming or going into the ranch?"

"No, I'd be afraid to go over there, after what happened at that evil place," Ester replied. "I still think about those young girls. I just can't believe what those men did to the girls."

"Yeah, I know, but it's good you didn't go over there," Fernando said. "I would stay away. I'll check it out this afternoon and let you know what I find, I promise. Be safe."

"Well, you be careful too, Mister Lopez. These are evil people."

Fernando's mind was racing as he hung up the phone. Maybe it was a long shot, but Three Hills Ranch just might be the key. He tried to remember how many of Warner's men were convicted and sentenced to the state penitentiary. Two underlings, as he recalled, and the man they called the Foreman, who managed the ranch. If Fernando remembered correctly, the underlings ended up with five-year sentences. The Foreman may have had a longer sentence, because he was the ranch supervisor and Warner's muscle.

Fernando booted up his computer and glanced at online calendars of previous years. By his calculation, at least two of Warner's men would have finished their sentences, the one exception being the Foreman. Maybe one or more of these men had come back to get revenge. That made sense, because he and Antonio were the ones who'd busted them and would be the ones they'd be after for payback. If he was out, the Foreman would be the most dangerous–a big muscular guy built like a lineman in the NFL, almost as big as Antonio. In fact, the Foreman had given Antonio all he could handle when the two of them finally clashed during the bust, which was saying a lot because Antonio was known as the SFPD enforcer, someone absolutely no one messed with.

Then he remembered the other law enforcement officer involved in the raid on Three Hills Ranch–Jodie Williams, a Santa Fe County Deputy Sheriff. Actually, Jodie had led the raid. He would need to warn both Jodie and Antonio about the possibility that one or more of Warner's men had come back for revenge. First, though, he wanted to check out Three Hills Ranch for himself. No need to worry Jodie and Antonio until he had a better idea of what the three of them were facing. The shooter may not even be connected to the Three Hills Ranch bust.

Fernando decided to skip lunch so he would have more time to investigate the ranch. He grabbed a bottle of water from his mini-fridge and locked up his office with the 'Closed' sign in the front window. He didn't plan on coming back today, no matter what he found at the ranch. The first thing he did when he climbed into his Cherokee was to make sure he had extra ammo in his glove compartment. He did, a new box of 41 Remington Magnum. Then he drove down to the Paseo and around to Old Santa Fe Trail, which took him to I-25 North. He took the interstate to Highway 285 South, which took him to Highway 41 South. He remembered how he'd met Jodie Williams here at the turn-off right before they busted the ranch.

Driving down Highway 41 toward the ancient village of Galisteo Fernando began to relax. The rolling hills and mesas were covered with yellow blooming chamisa and purple sage and smoky green grasses. He always wondered why so many people found the desert terrain ugly. To him this was the most beautiful landscape on the planet. Everything was subtle here, including the colors. No bright green in-your-face golf courses or designer suburban communities to smack your senses. Ancient Puebloans had lived here for thousands of years and yet had left virtually no footprint. Using local materials to build their pueblos, they had lived on and with the land and left hardly a mark. Outsiders with their expensive cars and re-remodeled mansions would never understand how sophisticated the Puebloans were.

Up ahead Fernando spotted a familiar grassy pull-off on the right side of the highway. He'd met Jodie here the first time they'd observed Three Hills Ranch. An old animal trail led from the road up to the top of the nearest of the three hills, from where they were able to observe the ranch below. Two of the young women being held captive at the ranch died trying to escape on this trail. He pulled over on the grass and weighed his options. He could climb the trail, or he could drive down to the dirt road that entered the ranch from the south. He decided the trail would be safer than driving right into the ranch, not knowing what to expect.

Fernando buckled on his holster and then walked to the rear compartment of the Cherokee and took out his Steyr. With his binoculars around his neck and his rifle in his hand, he stumbled down a small embankment and walked across a sandy ravine to a barbed wire fence. Once over the fence he found the familiar trail, a ribbon of dirt curving up to the top of the hill, maybe a half-mile away. Not such an easy hike lugging the Steyr and his binoculars.

He saw both animal and human footprints in the soft dirt of the trail as he climbed higher. Deer, elk, coyotes, and the most dangerous animal of all, humans. Hunters and hikers most likely, since the ranch had been idle for over five years now, abandoned and bound up in court with all of Warner's assets. The families of the young women held as sexual slaves at the ranch had been trying for years to get compensation. Like most of the filthy rich, Warner had hidden his fortune in trusts and foreign bank accounts that were difficult to crack.

Climbing with the rifle and binoculars tired him quickly. He stopped to rest on a large flat rock and then continued up the hill. When he reached the outcropping of rock on the crest, he stopped and leaned his rifle against the side of the tall rock. Then he scrambled down the other side of the hill to a boulder, from where he could observe the ranch with his binoculars. As soon as he trained the binoculars on the ranch he flashed back to the day of the raid, the day they rescued the captive women. The day ended with Warner dying in a fiery helicopter crash. When Fernando closed his eyes he could still see the copter bursting into flames against the hill and then Warner's charred body burned to a crisp on the helipad. It had become a recurring nightmare that had troubled his sleep since that day.

Fernando scanned the ranch with his binoculars, from Warner's four-sided mansion with the interior courtyard to the long wooden barracks where Warner kept the women captives. He studied the small guardhouse at the entrance of the dirt road and the helipad off to the side of the mansion, which still looked black and greasy from the explosion of Warner's helicopter. At first he saw nothing suspicious in the abandoned ranch. Then he spotted a white object off to the side of the barracks, partly obscured by the long veranda. A white car.

Suddenly Fernando saw movement over by the barracks. A door opened part way and then a man stepped out on the wooden porch. Short and thin as a rail, the man wore jeans and a baggy white T-shirt. Fernando focused his binoculars on the man's face but didn't recognize him. Might be one of Warner's former guards who had been sentenced to time in the state prison, but not the Foreman. He wasn't nearly big enough to be the Foreman.

Using his binoculars, Fernando followed the man in the white T-shirt as he walked across the yard to the guardhouse. The man appeared to be searching for something. When he came out of the guardhouse empty handed, the man walked directly to the mansion and entered through the front door. Fernando wondered if the man could be a caretaker of sorts hired by the court to look after the property while it was tied up in litigation.

Fernando lowered his binoculars and waited. Several long minutes later two men walked out of the mansion carrying blankets and other bedding. The man in the white T-shirt led the way, followed by none other than the Foreman. Fernando recognized him immediately: a big hulking man with huge shoulders and a wild head of hair, wearing khaki top to bottom. He looked even heavier than the day Antonio took him down after a brutal struggle.

Fernando remembered their fight as if it were only yesterday:

He and Antonio came across the Foreman in the basement of the mansion. The Foreman drew a knife and took off running down a long hallway. The Foreman made it halfway down the hall before Antonio tackled him from behind. The knife shot across the floor into the wall. The Foreman elbowed Antonio in the face, driving the big ex-Marine off momentarily. But Antonio grabbed the Foreman's leg as he tried to run off, pitching him face down on the floor. Both men hurled curses at each other.

On their feet now the two men faced off like boxers, sizing each other up. The Foreman struck first with a hard right hand, backing Antonio up. But as the Foreman moved forward, Antonio caught him with a vicious left uppercut to the chin that snapped the Foreman's head back. Antonio followed that with a straight right hand that dropped the Foreman to his knees.

Desperate, the Foreman reached for his holster, but before his hand could remove the revolver Antonio kicked him hard in the face, sending him crashing backwards on the floor, his nose spurting blood. The Foreman made one more attempt to reach his gun, but before he could Antonio rushed over and blocked him, kicking the gun out of his reach. Then Antonio stomped down hard on the outstretched arm, snapping bones. The Foreman screamed in pain.

Antonio deftly flipped the Foreman on his stomach and cuffed his hands behind his back, listening to the sound of the wounded man sputtering and choking on his own blood.

If only!

If the Foreman had choked to death on his own blood Fernando wouldn't be here now, two dead Santa Fe cops later, watching the Foreman and the other man carrying bedding materials out of the mansion. They placed the blankets and sheets on the porch and then went back inside the mansion, returning a few minutes later with boxes of kitchen supplies, assorted pots and pans, which they also deposited on the porch next to the bedding. Looked like they were picking up camping supplies for wherever they were hiding out.

While Fernando watched, the Foreman said something to the man in the white T-shirt, who nodded his head and walked off toward the white car. The man climbed into the car and drove it around to the mansion and popped the trunk. Together the Foreman and the man in the white T-shirt carried the boxes from the mansion to the trunk of the white car.

Just then Fernando shifted his weight, a big mistake. His knee knocked loose a small rock at the base of the boulder. He grabbed frantically for the rock with his left hand but missed. The rock rolled slowly down the hillside at first and then picked up speed, producing a shower of loose pebbles and sand. There was nothing he could do to prevent the inevitable. He could only watch the disaster unfold. He froze, feeling utterly helpless.

The shower of rocks sounded like a waterfall as it crashed onto the floor of the canyon.

Noticing the avalanche, the Foreman pointed to the boulder at the top of the hill. "Who's up there?" he shouted. Then he reached into the trunk of the white car and brought out a rifle. Looked like a semi-automatic assault weapon.

Fernando cursed himself for leaving the Steyr back at the outcropping of rock. Now what? He didn't have much choice when the Foreman started climbing the hill toward him.

Holding his binoculars against his chest, Fernando ducked low and scampered up the hill to the outcropping. Not low enough.

Thok! Thok! Thok!

The bullets ricocheted off the outcropping and sprayed Fernando with rock fragments. He slid on his hands and knees behind the big rock. He grabbed his Steyr and jacked a round into the chamber and then glanced down the hill at the advancing Foreman. He made a quick decision. Instead of returning fire, he turned and ran back down the trail toward the highway. Better to wait until he had more information, he told himself. And anyway, he didn't like the odds. The other guy wearing the white T-shirt had suddenly disappeared. The Foreman's accomplice could be circling around the hill to attack him from behind.

Even running with heavy gear, going down the hill was a lot easier than going up. He quickly made it to the flat rock where he had rested earlier. He knelt behind the rock and placed the Steyr on its flat surface, scanning the hill with his scope. If they came down the trail after him or around the mountain, they would be sitting ducks for the Steyr. He could pick them off one at a time.

He waited. And waited. Fifteen or twenty minutes went by and sill no one appeared on the hill. For whatever reason they hadn't come after him. He decided it was safe and headed for the Cherokee. As he walked away from the flat rock he heard a car coming up the highway slowly, heading north. He raised his binoculars and watched. Moments later he saw the car come into view, a white Audi sedan, not an Impala as Antonio thought. The two of them were in the car, with the Foreman at the wheel and the man with the white T-shirt riding shotgun. Both of them were craning their necks to look for him as they drove by, so Fernando squatted down in a patch of chamisa and sage until the car had passed.

Fernando returned to the flat rock to sit and rest for a moment. He felt both relief and dread. Relief that he now knew the identity of the shooter. And dread that the shooter had turned out to be the Foreman, one tough hombre.

At least he knew what the Foreman was driving, he told himself. That was a place to start.

6

Next morning Fernando called Jodie and Antonio to tell them the news. Neither answered, so he left messages about the Foreman and what he'd seen at Three Hills Ranch. Antonio called back within the hour.

"You're saying the shooter's our old friend the Foreman, eh?" Antonio asked. "Well, I can't say I'm surprised, he was one mean sonofabitch. I did some checking after I got your message. His legal name is Carter Hoover, from Douglas, Arizona. He was released from the New Mexico State Penitentiary this past June, a year early for good behavior. Go figure. Good behavior!"

Fernando laughed. "He knew how to play the game."

"Exactly," Antonio said. "So tell me, what's your plan? You think he'll go back to Three Hills Ranch?"

"I doubt it, now that he's been seen there," Fernando said. "Plus, it looked like he was getting supplies to take with him. Maybe to camp out or move in somewhere, I don't know."

"Which means he could be anywhere...or everywhere," Antonio said.

"Yeah...so be careful, Antonio," Fernando said. "This guy's dangerous."

"Hah! He's the one who should be careful," Antonio replied.

They agreed to contact each other with any news.

As soon as he clicked off Fernando began to worry that Antonio was taking the threat posed by the Foreman too lightly. Too much bravado could be a dangerous thing in this profession.

Still, he had made some progress, he reasoned.

Now that he knew the identity of the shooter and had alerted Jodie and Antonio, he should feel better, Fernando told himself. He had company; he wasn't alone. The three of them were a team. They had busted the Foreman once, and they could do it again. Yes?

Jodie finally called at half past ten. "Fernando, I got your message. I thought we locked that bastard up for at least seven years."

"We did," Fernando said, "but they let him out of the big house a year or so early for good behavior."

Jodie laughed. "That's funny. They must have a different idea of what constitutes good behavior."

"I just wanted to let you know that he's on the loose," Fernando said. "I got a call from Mrs. Hoke, who lives next to Three Hills Ranch. You might remember her and her husband, who Warner's men killed. She said she saw some activity at Three Hills and was worried the bad guys had returned. So I went out to check and sure enough the Foreman was there with another guy. Looked like they were loading up their car with bedding and other supplies from the mansion. I assume they must be camping or staying somewhere in the area."

"No kidding," Jodie said. "Well, that's the last thing I wanted to hear this morning."

"Well, be on the lookout for this Foreman guy, he's already killed two cops in Santa Fe and tried to kill both Antonio and me," Fernando said. "So what's up with you these days?"

"Yeah, I'm out here on the Old Las Vegas Highway," Jodie said. "We have a crime scene on the Shaggy Peak Trail. Seems a Santa Fe couple was robbed while hiking the trail. The husband's dead–shot in the head, execution style. And we think the wife was pushed off a cliff into a slot canyon that runs alongside the trail. We don't know if she's alive or dead."

"When did this happen?' Fernando asked.

"Yesterday evening, just before sunset," Jodie said. "Another hiker heard the shot and reported the crime. The husband was dead when we arrived. It was too dark to find the wife's body last night, but we're going to try again today. Wanna join us? Be like old times."

Fernando couldn't think of a reason to say no. Might get his mind off the Foreman. "Sure, I can be there in twenty minutes."

"I'll wait for you at the trailhead," she said and clicked off.

He had to think a moment about the location of the Shaggy Peak Trail. As best he remembered it was somewhere between Bobcat Bite and Apache Canyon. He grabbed another bottle of water, locked up his office, and climbed into the Cherokee. He drove down to the Paseo and around to Old Santa Fe Trail, which fed into the Old Las Vegas Highway.

Past I-25 the landscape changed: old city adobes gave way to sprawling subdivisions of frame and stucco houses, their lots manicured to picture perfect perfection. Only when he approached Bobcat Bite did the Santa Fe National Forest provide relief from the suburban sprawl. He slowed down when he passed Bobcat Bite, unsure of how far it was to the Shaggy Peak trailhead.

Further down Fernando spotted the sign marking the trailhead parking lot. Not a very popular trail with hikers, the parking lot was empty except for Jodie's Santa Fe County Sheriff's cruiser. Fernando pulled in beside the cruiser, noticing Jodie standing on a rise overlooking the parking lot. A tall athletic woman, a former University of New Mexico basketball player, she wore her uniform and reflecting sunglasses that gave her a slightly ominous look.

Fernando liked Jodie. A take-charge kind of cop, she had single-handedly brought down Warner's helicopter at Three Hills Ranch. She'd led their raid on Three Hills every step of the way, from their first visit to the bloody end. Fernando had great respect for her ever since.

Jodie waved at him from the rise. She looked about the same as Fernando remembered, maybe bulked up a bit in her chest and shoulders, which just added to her muscular stature.

Fernando left his Steyr locked in the rear of the Cherokee but kept his Smith & Wesson, since he had no idea what they would encounter. He climbed up the embankment and joined her on the rise.

"Good to see you, Jodie," he said.

They touched fists and stood looking at each other.

"You look good, Fernando," Jodie said. "I hear you retired and started your own private investigation business."

"I did, but it's turned out to be more of a hobby than a business because I never make any money," Fernando said, shaking his head. "Lotta *pro bono* work, as it turns out."

Jodie laughed. "I can imagine. You're a softy."

"Fill me in on this couple who were robbed–the dead husband and the missing wife."

Jodie nodded. "Let's walk. I'll tell you on the way up."

Fernando winced, knowing how fast Jodie hiked. Keeping up with her was always a problem. Nevertheless, he did his best to keep up as she shot up the trail into the foothills, through patches of piñon and juniper trees.

"From what we know the couple was robbed halfway up the trail by at least one armed man," Jodie said. "Victims were Richard and Joan Clark, both in their late forties. They'd only been married for a year or so. I'll show you the spot where the attack occurred. Looks like there was some sort of struggle. The husband ended up dead, shot in the back of his head. His wallet was taken, but nothing else–car keys, jewelry, whatever."

"What about the wife? You say she's missing?" Fernando asked, huffing and puffing behind her.

"Yeah, from the footprints and the crumbled side of the cliff, we think she either fell or was pushed off," Jodie said. "She fell into a slot canyon about a hundred feet deep. One of our guys–John Rodriguez, I don't know if you remember him–was able to climb down the cliff and look around, but he didn't see any sign of her, alive or dead. Too dark, even with a flashlight, to search the whole canyon. This morning we towed the Clarks' car to a police lot in town. A deputy checked their house on Don Gaspar Street just to make sure the wife hadn't caught a ride out of here and made it back somehow, but there was no one at home."

"Where's John now?" Fernando asked.

"He had to take off," Jodie said. "Bad accident on La Bajada Hill. They had to close Interstate Twenty-five south."

After that, Fernando fell further behind and their conversations soon ended. They climbed slowly up into the high country, marked by tall ponderosa pines that seemed to touch the sky. The trail ran along a series of deepening canyons to their left. Animal scat littered the trail. Deer, bobcat, bear, he could still recognize the droppings from the days of his youth when he would accompany his father and grandfather on hunting trips in the Pecos Wilderness. Memories flooded over him. Good memories, except he hadn't really enjoyed killing animals. He wondered if he would feel the same today. Probably so, since killing was something he did only when absolutely necessary and with lots of regrets, because he knew from a lifetime as a cop that when you kill someone they inevitably come back to haunt you.

After hiking for about an hour they approached a length of yellow caution tape staked along the trail for about twenty yards, blocking access. Jodie turned and waited for him to join her. "This is the crime scene. You can see where the ground is all torn up–that's where the husband and wife were attacked. Forensics collected blood stains and footprints."

Fernando nodded, still out of breath.

Jodie pointed to the edge of the cliff. "See where the cliff has crumbled? That's where the wife fell. If you get closer, you can see an embankment where she landed and slid down the bottom part of the cliff."

"What's back here?" Fernando asked, looking at another smaller area behind a boulder also cordoned off by yellow caution tape.

Jodie joined him. "That's where the husband was shot in the back of the head. We don't know if he was trying to run away or if they drug him over behind the rock and executed him."

Fernando spotted the dark stains on the sandy trail.

Jodie pointed up the mountain. About fifty yards from where they stood the slot canyon curved away from the trail. "See that slash in the rim? Looks like a stream running down from the mountain. Maybe we can follow the stream down into the canyon, what do you think?"

"Worth a try," Fernando said.

They continued up the trail, following the curve of the canyon. The stream turned out to be hardly more than a trickle of water, flowing and in some places dripping over a bed of rocks descending into the canyon.

"Be careful, some of the rocks look slippery," Jodie said.

They proceeded slowly, following a narrow, rocky animal path alongside the stream to the bottom of the canyon. They made it down without incident.

Jodie stopped to get her bearings, gauging the distance to where Joan Clark had fallen over the cliff. Then they made their way across the sand, through sparse patches of snake grass and prickly pear cactus. Further down they came to a rough spot in the sand, churned up by human footprints and indentations where Joan Clark most likely had landed and clawed furiously with her hands. All of which indicated she was still alive after she landed. After that, who knew?

Jodie pointed to the top of the cliff. "You can see where she fell over the rim and landed on that outcropping of sand, then slid down to the bottom here. Looks like she survived the fall."

Fernando nodded. "Yeah, the sandy ledge saved her life," he said, already searching for Joan Clark's footprints leading away from where she landed after sliding down the slope. "Here," he said, motioning to the ground. "Small sneaker, a woman's size, walking south."

"But the entrance is to the north," Jodie said.

Fernando led the way, noticing small drops of blood as he followed the footprints, which circled south around the canyon floor and then reversed directions and headed north. The injured woman had been trying to find a way out of the canyon. Which she apparently did, because her tracks ended at the rocks on the far side of the stream. She'd climbed out of the canyon the same way they had entered, just on the other or western side of the stream.

"At this point she's bleeding, but alive," Jodie said.

"Yeah, but where is she now, that's the question," Fernando added.

They hiked up the rough trail on the western side of the stream, scouring the rocks as they climbed. They found traces of blood on a large rock, where the injured woman may have stopped for a breather, but nothing else. At the top they stopped to consider their options.

"She may have wondered off in the darkness, who knows," Fernando said. "She could have been dazed from her fall. Even soft sand can knock the wind out of a person and disrupt their thinking."

They searched the area around the mouth of the canyon for over half an hour, combing the grounds thoroughly and finding no trace of the woman. Finally they gave up and returned to the Shaggy Peak Trail leading down the mountain.

"What do you think?" Jodie asked.

Fernando shook his head. "I don't know. If she's not at home, she must be here somewhere. You may have to do an air search, turn it over to the choppers and see what they can find."

Jodie shook her head, not liking the sound of that. "I don't know, we're stretched so thin."

They started down the mountain, their eyes searching the tall ponderosa pines off to their left. A few minutes later Fernando noticed a primitive forest road visible through the trees. They'd missed the road on their way up, when they were more concerned with what was in the canyon. Along the road Fernando saw a scattering of homemade signs painted on wood and nailed to trees. The signs warned of bears, telling hikers to keep away.

"I didn't know there were many bears this close to the highway," Fernando said. "This is quite a ways from the ski basin and the higher country."

Jodie stopped and studied the signs. "Let's take a look."

They left the trail and walked along the road. When they'd gone about forty yards they saw a structure of some sort among the ponderosa pines. The structure turned out to be a primitive log cabin with a flat roof and discolored logs covered with moss and wood rot. Out front of the cabin sat an enormous pile of firewood spread out in a semi-circle. In the middle of the semi-circle stood the remains of a large tree trunk with an axe sunk deep into its top.

The door of the tumbledown cabin hung open at an odd angle. They were about to take a closer look when suddenly a barrel of a man stepped out of the door. With huge shoulders and a long shaggy beard, the man wore a black fur cap and vest that looked like the fur of a black bear. Around his neck dangled a chain attached to a real bear paw with two-inch nails, hacked off at the joint. The man looked agitated and disoriented. He behaved like a wild animal protecting his den, threatened by invaders. They were the invaders.

Growling, the bear claw man rushed for the axe. He grabbed the axe handle and yanked it out of the tree stump. Then he swung the axe wildly over his head and came at them.

7

Fernando and Jodie stood side by side watching the bear claw man dance erratically while swinging the axe over his head. Dancing, he moved closer and closer to them. Finally he stopped and turned to face them. Then, with a howl, he charged through the pine needles toward them, holding the axe straight out in front of him like a lance. He looked absolutely psychotic, as if he were in some deep delusional trance far removed from reality.

Jodie's right hand touched her holster. Then she extended her left hand, palm out. "Sir, if you come any closer with that axe, I'll have to shoot you," she said flatly, without emotion. Her voice conveyed the message that she didn't care if she shot him or not, it was up to him.

The bear claw man stopped and lowered his axe but still held it tightly in his hand.

By Fernando's calculations the man was about twenty yards away, far enough away that Jodie could shoot the sonofabitch before he released the axe.

"Okay, now drop it," Jodie said, pulling out her weapon.

The bear claw man dropped his axe. "What do you want?" he asked gruffly.

"We need your help," Jodie said, softening her tone. "We want to ask you some questions about what happened on the trail yesterday afternoon."

The bear claw man stared at Jodie, mute.

"Did you see the man who was murdered on the trail?" Jodie asked. "Or the man's wife, who fell into the canyon?"

"The bears got 'em," the bear claw man said. "I warned 'em. I got signs all over here telling people to stay way. The bears are dangerous."

"Did you see the murderer, the person who attacked them?" Jodie asked.

The bear claw man shook his head. "No, but I heard them yellin'."

"Them? How many of them were there?" Jodie asked.

"The woman and two, maybe three men," the bear claw man said. "They raised quite a ruckus. Then I heard a gunshot and the woman screamin' bloody murder. Then nothing. Bears got 'em all, I reckon."

Fernando stepped forward and asked, "What about you? If the bears are so dangerous, what are you doing here?"

"I got no problem with the bears," the bear claw man said. "Bears are my spirit animals. I can talk to them. They leave me alone and I leave them alone. It's the strangers that come by who are in danger. Like you."

Fernando shrugged. "I'll take my chances."

"You best be getting out of here now," the bear claw man said. "The bears heard you, I can tell. They hear everything. They'll be coming any time now."

The way the bear claw man spoke while cranking his neck up and down and all around spooked Fernando. The man looked unstable, as if he were hearing voices and the voices were telling him to do very bad things.

Jodie put her weapon in its holster. "At the moment we're looking for the woman. Apparently she fell into the canyon, but she's not down there now. That means she must have survived the fall and walked out. Or someone found her and helped her out. Maybe you. So I'm asking you again, have you seen her?"

Bear claw man shook his head from side to side.

Jodie looked over at the man's cabin. "Do you mind if we take a look in your cabin?"

"No!" he shouted.

"In that case we'll be back tomorrow with a search warrant and maybe a warrant for your arrest," Jodie said, stretching the truth a bit.

Bear claw man quickly reconsidered. "Okay...but don't touch anything!" he said.

Fernando followed Jodie and bear claw man through the ponderosa pines to the cabin. He noticed an outhouse behind the cabin and a well with a hand pump off to the side. Clearly the cabin had no running water or electricity.

Bear claw man held the door wide open for Jodie but then stepped in front of Fernando.

Fernando let them go in first and then opened the door for himself, surprised to find the door attached to the jam by means of leather straps. Inside he saw Jodie make a beeline for a table and chair in the corner of the small cabin, where she examined a first aid kit open on the table and a pile of bandages, some of them bloody, in a nearby waste basket. Tape, gauze pads, and a bottle of rubbing alcohol remained on the table, next to a pair of scissors.

Jodie turned to face bear claw man. "You want to explain these bloody bandages?"

Bear claw man shook his shaggy head. "I cut my hand last week. It's all healed now."

"That's a lot of blood for a cut on your hand that's already healed," Jodie said, taking a latex glove and a plastic bag out of her rear pocket. Then she picked a bloody bandage out of a nearby wastebasket and deposited it in the plastic bag, which she tucked in her duty belt.

While they argued Fernando looked around the one-room cabin. An army cot with sleeping bag on top served as a bedroom. Two canvas lawn chairs and an overturned cardboard box occupied the middle of the room, while the kitchen consisted of a counter on which sat a water bucket, tin plates and utensils, and an old camping stove. Under the counter a cheap Styrofoam cooler had been buried in the dirt floor to take the place of a refrigerator. A kerosene lantern and two battery operated Coleman lanterns hung from two-by-fours nailed to the log walls. Rustic didn't even begin to describe this dump, Fernando thought.

Jodie was ready to leave by the time he finished snooping. She turned and walked out of the cabin without bothering to say a word to bear claw man. Fernando hurried after her.

"What do you think?" Fernando asked as they started down the trail.

"Looks suspicious," Jodie said. "Forensics has samples of Joan Clark's blood. We'll know in a day or so if the blood on this bandage is a match. My guess is affirmative."

"That would mean he either helped her escape or is holding her captive somewhere," Fernando added.

"Exactly."

As before, Fernando had trouble keeping up with Jodie on the way down, which was faster but harder on the knees than going up. By the time they reached the parking lot at the trailhead, Fernando's knees ached like hell.

Jodie checked her watch. "It's almost two o'clock. You want to stop at Bobcat Bite for a late lunch? It might not be gourmet, but it's close."

"Sounds good," Fernando said.

"I'll meet you there," Jodie said, and jumped into her cruiser and took off quickly down the highway.

On the other hand Fernando took his sweet time, massaging his knees for a while before climbing in the Cherokee. Parched, he drank more than half of his bottle of water and tried to catch his breath. Whenever he worked with Jodie he felt like an old man, out of shape and out of place. But Jodie was a thirty-year-old former athlete from the University of New Mexico. What did he expect?

Fernando pulled out on the Old Las Vegas Highway and drove slowly down to Bobcat Bite. He parked next to Jodie's cruiser in front of the brown stucco building, the only vehicles in the parking lot at this odd hour. As soon as he stepped outside he saw Jodie waving at him from the patio on the west side of the building. He walked the length of the long building to the patio, surrounded by a waist-high stone fence with a flagstone entrance.

Jodie sat at one of the front tables under a white umbrella, where she had a clear view of the highway and the parking lot. She motioned for him to grab one of the black metal chairs.

Fernando pulled up a chair and sat across the table from Jodie. "Nice patio. I haven't been here in years."

Just then a waitress came out of the restaurant door and approached the table. "Welcome back, Jodie," she said with a big smile, a skinny older woman with her hair tied back.

"Thanks, Claire," Jodie said.

Claire dropped off menus and went back inside the restaurant.

Fernando watched the waitress walk away and then turned to Jodie. "Do you come here frequently?"

Jodie nodded. "Yeah, we live nearby on Nine Mile Road. Sharon likes the patio, so we come here a lot during the summer and fall. Not so much in the winter. Inside's kind of cramped."

Claire returned momentarily, not having any customers to serve. "Do you know what you want? No hurry. I'm just trying to keep busy."

"I'll have the green chile cheeseburger with iced tea," Jodie said.

"I'll have the same," Fernando added.

Claire wrote down their orders. "You must be working today," she said to Jodie with a big smile.

"Yeah, we just came from the Shaggy Peak Trail where a man was murdered yesterday," Jodie said. "We ran into this strange guy dressed up like a bear living in an old derelict cabin. Do you know anything about him?"

The waitress sighed. "That's Johnny Roybal. He's a hermit. He was mauled by a bear a few years ago and hasn't been the same since. Thinks he's a bear after the mauling. He's a little touched, if you know what I mean."

Jodie laughed. "Touched. We know what you mean."

Fernando couldn't resist. "So what, he thinks he became a bear after the mauling, like the victim of a vampire becomes a vampire?"

Claire laughed. "Something like that. I think he's from somewhere up by Taos. He's always lived in the woods."

"Does he ever come here?" Jodie asked. "I mean to order food?"

"Once in a while," Claire said. "He'll come in for an early dinner, when no one else is here. I don't think he likes to be around people much...."

Later, after finishing their burgers, they ordered coffee. When it arrived, Jodie leaned back in her chair and stared at Fernando. "Do you really think this Foreman guy has come back to Santa Fe looking for revenge?"

"Looks like it," Fernando said. "He's killed two cops so far and now seems to be targeting Antonio and me. Maybe you, too, since you were in charge of the raid that busted him. And you killed Warner."

"Never ends, does it?" Jodie asked. "You bust a perp, you lock him up, and a few years later he gets out and comes after you. Incarceration's a joke these days. The goddamned judges are much too lenient."

Fernando nodded. "I agree, and it seems to get worse every year. I don't know if the Foreman will target you, but I would be on guard. If you see a suspicious white sedan tailing you, give me a call ASAP."

"Oh, I'll be careful," Jodie said. "But I for damn sure won't tell Sharon. She'll be hollering for me to get a different occupation. Every time something like this comes up, she wants me to resign."

"Estelle's the same way," Fernando added. "She wants me to give up my private eye business."

Jodie pushed her coffee cup away, disgusted. "Tell you the truth, I would like nothing better than to put a bullet right between the Foreman's eyes. Then we wouldn't have to worry about him being released for good behavior. Good behavior, what a friggin' joke!"

Fernando smiled.

Jodie stood up and placed a twenty dollar bill on the table. "If the Foreman does come after me, he's a dead man."

8

Fernando waved goodbye as Jodie drove off fast on the Old Las Vegas Highway, heading east toward Pecos, where she had another appointment. He worried she, like Antonio, was taking the news about the Foreman too lightly, but what could be do? He felt stuffed after a big, mid-afternoon meal, not his normal routine. He liked to eat only one big meal a day: dinner. Estelle called him obsessive-compulsive. Maybe, but so what? He just liked his routines.

Wishing he could take a nap instead, Fernando climbed into the Cherokee and pulled out on the highway. He drove his usual five miles an hour below the speed limit. He'd driven only a few miles toward Santa Fe when he spotted a white ghost behind him, a slender white sedan that went in and out of sight as he drove over the hills and around the curves. He tried to drive and watch the rear view mirror at the same time and ended up swerving out of his lane. The blaring horn of an oncoming motorist brought his attention back to the road.

When he checked again the white sedan seemed to have disappeared. Had he imagined it, a figment of his imagination, not to mention his paranoia? Then out of nowhere the white ghost came speeding up behind him. For a moment it looked like the sedan intended to rear-end him or drive him off the road. Just as suddenly the sedan braked and fell further behind the Cherokee.

Fernando cursed out loud. He'd had enough of the driver toying with him. He could only assume it was the Foreman.

Making a quick decision, he slowed the Cherokee looking for a wide shoulder along the highway. He pulled over as soon as he spotted a shoulder wide enough for the Cherokee. When he came to a stop he took his Smith & Wesson out of its holster and placed it on the center console. Then he turned to face the highway, daring the Foreman to stop.

Suddenly Fernando heard the roar of a big engine. The white ghost flashed by him going at least eighty or ninety miles per hour, way too fast for a two-lane highway. Fernando pulled out on the highway and followed, falling farther and farther behind. It looked like the white ghost intended to race into Santa Fe, but instead it turned left at Exit 284 and jumped over to I-25 South, disappearing quickly into the traffic and the rolling hills.

Fernando didn't follow. He continued down the highway to Old Santa Fe Trail. There was no way in hell he could ever catch a speedy Audi driving his lumbering Cherokee.

He realized he'd been gripping the steering wheel so tight his hands were numb. He shook them one at a time to get some feeling back in them. His nerves were shot. He realized once again that he was getting too old for this. He took a few deep breaths and tried to calm down. He started to feel better as he drove down Old Santa Fe Trail, seeing the familiar adobes with their colorful sunflowers and hollyhocks out front. Back on his terrain.

Fernando turned right on the Paseo and followed it around to Canyon Road. He decided to go directly to his office to recoup, maybe call Antonio and Manny to let them know what happened. Halfway up he had second thoughts and instead pulled into the parking lot across the street from El Farol. It was early, barely four o'clock, but he needed something to calm his nerves.

He walked across Canyon Road to the remodeled El Farol, its tan stucco trimmed with dark brown wood looking spiffy in the afternoon light. He stepped up onto the porch and through the front door into the cozy restaurant. A couple old timers who he didn't know hunkered down at the bar nursing their beers. One of the afternoon bartenders named Penny waved at him from behind the bar.

"Hey, Penny," he said.

With a sheepish grin, Penny pointed to the restaurant part of El Farol. "The crowd's all down there."

That's when he saw the celebration. At first Fernando didn't understand. A large portrait of Wayne Fontenot painted by his long deceased friend and fellow painter Tommy Macaroni sat on an easel just inside the walkway into the restaurant. Inside, stacked against the walls of the spacious room were some of Wayne's paintings, crude splashes of bright colors on canvas depicting (sort of) Santa Fe buildings and landscapes. He thought momentarily that El Farol was sponsoring a sale of Wayne's paintings to raise money for the old rascal.

Then he saw Ruby. She had tears in her eyes. She was actually crying, only the second time he'd seen her cry. It reminded him of how she had raged and blamed him for the death of Jimmy Mackey, her ex-husband.

For not protecting Jimmy from the gunmen who killed him in Taos.

Ruby didn't say a word. She walked across the room and hugged him. "He's gone, Fernando. His nurse called me just before Noon. She found him in his chair. Just stopped breathing."

"I'm sorry, Ruby," Fernando said, holding her tight.

Finally she pulled away. "Well, shit...what are you gonna do?" she asked, wiping her face with a tissue.

Fernando sighed. "Nothing you can do." He looked around the room and saw the motley collection of Wayne friends who had come to remember him on this day of his passing: Blaine Rogers, the owner of the Picasso and Co. Gallery that had tried for decades to sell Wayne's paintings; Dave Stein, another painter who was almost as old as Wayne; Athena Loering, the owner of Athena Gallery, accompanied by her boy-toy Sonny Davis; and a host of other ne'er do wells who Fernando recognized but didn't know personally. The Canyon Road crowd, all of them either artists or gallery owners. Wayne's friends.

Several tables had been moved together, forming one long banquet table cluttered with glasses and pitchers of beer. It was a hard-drinking crowd, and they were there to celebrate Wayne.

Blaine rose to speak first, as Fernando pulled up a chair. Blaine wore his typical outfit: a T-shirt, red Bermuda shorts, and a fishing vest. "Well, hell, I don't know what to say about the old bastard. He lived the way he wanted to live, painted whenever he felt like it and as far as I know never did a day's work in his life. We should all be so lucky, eh?"

The miscreants all cheered as Blaine continued. "I want you all to know I'm feeling a little guilty today for not taking more of Wayne's work at my gallery, as awful as it was. I know, I know, I should have taken more of his paintings, even though the last painting of Wayne's I was able to sell was back in 1999, to a drunk Texan who needed a gift for his wife to make up for some indiscretion he was guilty of. Hah! Imagine the wife's reaction when she saw one of Wayne's ghastly paintings!"

Everyone laughed.

Ruby rose next to eulogize her fallen friend. "Well, I never thought I'd say it, but I miss the old crank. I've been bringing him meals for months now and keeping his house clean, and every time he saw me he would refer to me as Claude, his long lost imaginary lover from the nineteen seventies. As if Claude would ever have anything to do with a prickly old crank like Wayne. Still, I miss him. I'm going to miss seeing him every afternoon at El Farol. Say what you will about Wayne, he could keep you entertained with all his crazy ideas."

"Amen!" someone yelled at the end of the table, maybe Sonny.

Next Dave Stein rose unsteadily on his feet. The tiny shrunken old man wore his best suit, purchased at the old Sears store on Lincoln Avenue decades ago. Dave talked out of the side of his mouth, like a ventriloquist, so when he talked you were always looking for the dummy.

"He was a man for all that," Dave said, and then sat down.

"What...did he just quote the Bard?" Blaine asked.

Athena raised her hand, a heavy-set woman with glasses and gray hair. "He pestered me so much that I bought one of his paintings this past winter," she said, speaking from her chair. "Dark, dreary globs of paint... supposed to be the cathedral, I think. I just put it away in my storeroom because I could never sell it. I just marked it up to charity."

"Which was good, because I would never hang it in the gallery," Sonny added. "It would scare away our customers."

Everyone laughed, including Ruby.

Smiling, Fernando sat back in his chair and took it all in: the camaraderie, the cold beer, the incessant chatter and the bad jokes. It was almost enough to make him forget the white ghost waiting for him somewhere outside the door of El Farol.

9

Fernando didn't make it to his office until nearly eleven o'clock. Too many beers yesterday afternoon at El Farol. Ruby still hadn't shown up at her gallery next door, probably recovering from the melee that broke out at the end of Wayne's memorial celebration. When the bartender told them the tables had to be moved back to get ready for the dinner crowd, Ruby asked Blaine to take Wayne's paintings to his gallery for a posthumous show. That set off Blaine, who not only refused but told Ruby to toss the paintings in the trash bins out in the alley. The bartender had to step in to separate the two and ended up tossing both of them out. Fernando and the rest of the celebrants skulked out one at a time.

He still hadn't told Antonio and Manny about his encounter with the white ghost. He grabbed his cell phone and was about to call Antonio when he had a change of heart. What's the rush? He could call this afternoon when he felt better. So he put his feet up on his desk and read the morning *Independent*. He started with the first section, reading the crime news and a long article about how various interest groups were already fighting about what to include and what to exclude from the upcoming Fiesta. He'd just turned to the sports page when he heard the crunch of gravel outside. Someone was walking down the path to his office.

Through the window he saw a small person wearing what appeared to be a hoody stepping up to his door. The person knocked.

"Come in," Fernando yelled, taking his Smith & Wesson out of its holster, just in case. The person at the door was much too small to be the Foreman, but the Foreman could have sent someone else to do his dirty work.

The door opened and in walked a tiny woman wearing a scarf over her head and sunglasses. Apparently the lady didn't want to be recognized walking into the office of a private dick. He put his Smith & Wesson back in its holster.

"Mr. Lopez?" the woman asked.

"That's me," he said. "What can I do for you?"

The woman sat in the chair across from his desk and removed her sunglasses and scarf. A tiny blonde with scratches and bruises on her face and arms. Not even heavy make-up covered the wounds on her cheeks and forehead. Looked like she'd been in a bad automobile accident. Something about her looked familiar, in spite of her present condition. Fernando tried his best to place her but came up empty. He couldn't look past her cuts and bruises.

"You probably don't remember me," she said. "I'm Joan Clark, the woman whose husband was murdered out in Apache Canyon."

Fernando's head cleared instantly. "You're kidding! Everyone's looking for you, not knowing if you were dead or alive!"

Joan nodded. "When we first met many years ago my name was Joan Novak, my maiden name. I was the nurse who took care of the girls at Three Hills Ranch for Robert Warner. Remember?"

"Of course, that's where I've seen you," Fernando said, his spirits sinking. He couldn't seem to get away from Three Hills Ranch. Once again it all came back to him in a rush, the whole sordid story of the young girls sexually abused by Warner and the pedophiles he flew in on his helicopter. Working with Jodie, he and Antonio had busted Novak along with the other workers at the ranch. But Novak claimed to be only trying to help the girls and the Prosecutor believed her. She'd pled out, agreeing to testify against the Foreman and the others for a lighter sentence.

Fernando could never decide if Novak was telling the truth. She may have thought she was helping the girls, but if so she had a damn funny way of helping. He remained dubious.

Joan straitened up in her chair. "You probably know that I accepted a plea deal in exchange for my testimony against Warner's foreman and his other guards, or whatever you call them. I served a year in prison and another year on probation. I didn't lose my nurse's license, though. I'm working now at Presbyterian Urgent Care on Saint Michael's Drive."

Fernando frowned. "Okay, I remember, but where have you been the last day or so? Everyone's been looking for you, including the Santa Fe County Sheriff. They didn't know where you were or if you were even alive."

Joan sighed. "I know. I'm sorry about that, but I didn't want to go to the police because of my record. I remembered you seemed...well...more understanding than most of the others. So I decided to come to you."

"Me? What can I do for you?" Fernando asked.

"I'm afraid," Joan said. "The person who killed my husband was Carter Hoover, the man they called the Foreman at Three Hills Ranch.

He's back in town and wants to get even with me for testifying against him."

Fernando interrupted her. "He's also killed two cops in Santa Fe and attempted to kill another...and me."

Joan seemed taken aback by the news. She paused for a moment and said, "So then you know he's back in town. We didn't know, my husband and I. We saw this white car driving by our house several times. Seemed suspicious. Then on our way to hike the Shaggy Peak Trail a couple of days ago my husband saw the white car following us. Richard said not to worry because the car drove on by the trailhead instead of following us into the parking lot. So we hiked up the trail about three-quarters of the way to the top and then turned back, because it was getting late. We'd gone a short distance when we saw two men coming toward us on the trail. I recognized Carter right away because of his khaki uniform and the way he rolls up his shirt sleeves over his big muscles. Real macho like."

"Did he recognize you?" Fernando asked.

"Of course," Joan said. "He knew who I was. He confronted me right away, said I'd betrayed him and the others. I'd ratted them out and now I had to pay, he said. Then he grabbed my arm and twisted it. My husband tried to intervene but the other guy hit him in the face with a pistol. Before I could help him Carter and the other guy drug my husband behind some rocks and shot him. I screamed, but there was no one else on the trail to help. To stop me from screaming Carter ran over and pushed me over the side of the cliff. Then he laughed. I could hear him laughing as I fell backward. He's always been sadistic like that."

"We saw where you fell," Fernando said. "You might remember Jodie from Three Hills Ranch? She and I hiked into the canyon looking for you yesterday. We had no idea you were the former Joan Novak. So how did you survive the fall? And how did you get out of the canyon in the dark?"

"It's a long story," Joan said, shaking her head. "When I fell, I hit some kind of sandy ledge and rolled down the slope over rocks and bushes. That's where I got all these cuts and bruises. I landed on my back with the wind knocked out of me. It took me a while to come to my senses. I was confused, and it was getting dark in the canyon. After a few minutes I managed to sit up. I could feel the blood on my arms and legs but couldn't do anything about it. I found my cell phone and tried to call a friend, but there was no service in the canyon. Finally I heard the roar of a wild animal, a big animal. Scared me to death, especially when I saw this furry black creature coming toward me out of the shadows. It took me a while to realize it was a man dressed in black fur, not a bear."

"Yeah, we ran into him too," Fernando said, interrupting her narrative. "His name's Johnny Roybal. He's a little mental, I'm told."

"He scared me to death when I first saw him," Joan said. "I tried to run away from him but he caught me and held me until I calmed down. Took me a few minutes to get my senses back. When I did I realized he was trying to help, not hurt me."

"He didn't try to hold you captive?" Fernando asked.

"No, he actually saved me," Joan said. "Took me a while, but when I started to get my strength back he helped me walk up the trail to his cabin at the top of the canyon. In the cabin he cleaned my cuts and scrapes and applied bandages to the bigger wounds. He didn't talk much, a strange fellow wearing all that fur. I was exhausted and fell asleep on an old army cot. I didn't wake up until the first light of morning. I looked around, but the strange man had gone off somewhere, I didn't see him. So I got my things together and left. I walked down the trail to the parking lot. My car had been towed away, so I didn't know what to do. Fortunately my cell phone was working in the parking lot, so I called a good friend, a nurse who works with me at Urgent Care. She picked me up and I've been staying with her ever since. I'm scared to go home, because Carter knows where I live."

"That's quite a story," Fernando said.

"I wanted you to know that he's in town...but I guess you already knew," Joan said.

"Yes, and so do the County Sheriff and the Santa Fe Police Department," Fernando said. "If I were you, I would stay with your friend until he's arrested. I wouldn't even go to work, just lay low. He's already killed your husband and tried to kill you. We should catch up with him soon, hopefully."

Joan nodded. "I will."

"By the way, did the Foreman give you any idea where he might be staying?" Fernando asked.

"No, not exactly. He mentioned Three Hills, said it looked mighty deserted thanks to people like me, whatever that means," Joan said. "He seems to blame me for what happened to Robert Warner. For everything, really."

Fernando nodded. "Well, I wouldn't take anything he says seriously. But yeah, one of the neighbors down there called me claiming to have seen or heard someone at Three Hills Ranch, so I went down to check it out. And sure enough, it was the Foreman. I saw him and another guy, a tall, skinny fellow wearing a white T-shirt."

"Yes, that's the man who was with Carter on the trail," Joan said.

"I'm not surprised," Fernando said.

"It's funny, but the strange man dressed like a bear said he'd seen the two men who attacked me before," Joan said. "I don't know how reliable this bear guy is, but he said he knew where they were staying," Joan said.

"Really? How would he know?"

Joan shrugged.

Fernando took one of his cards out of his desk. "Here's my card. Call me anytime if you see him again or can think of anything you forgot to tell me."

"Thanks."

Fernando pushed a note pad across the desk to her. "Write down your cell phone number and the name and address of the person you're staying with. I'll let you know as soon as we catch up to him."

Joan wrote the information on the pad and then stood next to the desk for a moment. She started to say something but then stopped. Instead, she turned and walked away.

"I'll be in touch," Fernando said as she stepped out of the office.

10

Fernando spent what remained of the morning brooding about Joan and what she had told him. He now suspected the Foreman had three specific targets in addition to himself: Antonio, Jodie, and now Joan. He didn't know what to make of Joan's story about the bear claw man. When he first encountered the bear claw man, Fernando thought he was a dangerously deranged, anti-social loner, someone like the notorious Unabomber. But Joan said the bear claw man had saved her–helped her out of the canyon after she had fallen and even tended to her wounds. That sounded like a Good Samaritan, not a Unabomber.

As Noon approached Fernando decided to go next door and ask Ruby if she wanted to go to El Farol for lunch. His cell phone rang before he could lock up. When he saw Estelle was calling he answered immediately, worried. She never called him during the day. Only in emergencies.

"Fernando, I decided to go home for lunch, but when I got there I found a white car in our driveway," Estelle said. "It looked suspicious, so I drove on by. What do you know about this? What aren't you telling me?"

"What kind of white car?" Fernando asked, beginning to panic.

"I don't know, just a small white sedan," Estelle said. "Looked like a foreign make."

Fernando locked the door and rushed to his Cherokee, still talking on the phone. "I'll tell you later. Just stay away from the house. I'm on my way now."

He hung up before Estelle could ask more questions. Better she didn't know the full story.

Fernando raced down to the Paseo and over to Acequia Madre. He slowed down when he saw the white ghost at the end of his driveway, trying to decide how best to play this.

The Foreman made the decision for him. The white ghost spun around in the middle of Acequia Madre and raced past him down to the Paseo.

Fernando caught a blurred glimpse of the Foreman at the wheel and another man in the passenger's seat as they sped by. He pulled into his driveway and spun the Cherokee around to follow. By the time he turned left on the Paseo the white ghost was turning left on Old Santa Fe Trail at the bottom of the hill. He followed as best he could, slowed first by a red light at the intersection and then by slow traffic on Old Santa Fe Trail. Finally he lost sight of the Audi altogether, but picked it up again as he approached the ramps to I-25.

Not slowing down, the Foreman swerved onto the entrance ramp to I-25 South. Fernando followed, turning right onto the ramp in hot pursuit. The Cherokee's speedometer hit eighty and then ninety miles per hour and still he fell farther and farther behind the white ghost. He quickly lost contact with the super fast Audi, which he reckoned had to be going well over one hundred miles per hour. There was no way a Cherokee could catch an Audi on an open highway.

Moments later as Fernando approached the Cerrillos Road exit he saw the white ghost weaving in and out of traffic on Cerrillos Road below. By the time he turned onto Cerrillos the Foreman was long gone, so Fernando slowed down and took in the many cluttered sights of Cerrillos Road. When he saw Café Castro ahead, one of his favorite restaurants, he decided to stop for takeout. Castro's was starting to get crowded, but he found a server at the front counter and ordered his usual, chicken enchiladas with red chile. The server, Annie, was too busy to chat, so left a twenty dollar bill on the counter and left.

Outside, Fernando climbed into the Cherokee and placed his lunch on the passenger's seat. Before starting the engine he sat in the Cherokee for a few minutes pondering his situation. The Foreman was playing mind games with the four of them. Trying–and doing a pretty damn good job of it–to intimidate them. They found themselves waiting for the Foreman's next move. Somehow they needed to change that calculus and become the hunters instead of the hunted. But how?

The question was even more urgent now that the Foreman knew where he and Joan and probably Jodie lived. Maybe not Antonio, because the big man lived off grid in the Pecos Wilderness.

Fernando decided to take the rest of the day off and not return to his office this afternoon. So he drove to the Paseo and around to Acequia Madre. Estelle wouldn't be home for several hours, so he had time to check his fortifications and make some phone calls. Since their small one-car garage only had room for Estelle's Camry, he parked the Cherokee beside the garage, close to the house, and retrieved his Steyr from the rear compartment. Then he locked and set the alarm on the Cherokee and hurried into the house carrying the Steyr in one hand and his lunch in the other hand.

The first thing Fernando did on entering the house was take the Steyr out of its case and lean it against his office desk, easy access from any part of the house. Then he sat down at the kitchen table and ate his lunch. After lunch he made the rounds, checking all the windows to make sure they were locked. No one used what was once the front door anymore because it faced a stand of cottonwoods, not the street. Instead they used the kitchen door, which opened on their patio and driveway. Even though the unused front door hadn't been opened in years, he double bolted it anyway, just to make sure no one could enter without making a lot of noise. Then he checked his security system. They used it rarely and only when they left for vacations. Tonight, before they went to bed, he would activate the system.

Estelle didn't like him to wear his holster inside the house, but today she would have to make an exception. He'd had it on all day and planned to keep it on until he went to bed, when he would place his Smith & Wesson on the nightstand.

Fernando figured the Foreman would come up the driveway, if and when he came. That meant he would confront the Foreman from the kitchen, so he placed extra ammo in the kitchen's utility drawer, just in case. That's about all he could do in terms of preparations–at least at this point.

That done, Fernando sat at the kitchen table and called Manny and then Antonio with his cell phone. He filled them in on recent developments, including what he'd learned from the reappearance of Joan Clark, aka Novak: that it was the Foreman who had pushed her over the cliff and the bear claw man who had found her in the canyon and helped her recover from her fall. Fernando also told them that the bear claw man claimed to have seen the Foreman and to know where the Foreman and his companion were hiding.

Then Fernando called Jodie and relayed the same information he'd told Manny and Antonio. By this time he was talking too fast and apparently not making much sense to Jodie.

Immediately Jodie asked for clarification. "Let me get this straight. You're saying the woman we've been searching for, who happens to be the nurse from Three Hills Ranch, is hiding at a friend's house because she's afraid of the man who pushed her over the cliff, who happens to be the Foreman from Three Hills Ranch, is that correct?" she asked.

"Yes," Fernando said.

"Well, that's going to be a problem, because we can't close the missing person case unless we interview her," Jodie said. "Can you at least give me the name and contact information for Joan's friend?"

"I really can't," Fernando said. "It was given to me in confidence. She's afraid the Foreman will find her if she comes out of hiding."

"But damnit, Fernando, I need that information in order to do my job," Jodie replied.

"Tell you what, I'll ask Joan Clark to contact you, if she's willing to go public. How's that?"

"Not good, but it sounds like it's the best I'm going to get from you," Jodie said.

Fernando changed the subject. "By the way, there's something else I wanted to mention. Joan told me the bear claw man said he'd seen the Foreman before and knew where he was staying."

Jodie didn't respond.

"Did you hear me?" Fernando asked.

"Yeah, but how is that possible?" Jodie asked. "First of all, he's a nut case. Second, he's a hermit. He lives alone on the mountain. I didn't even see any means of transportation at his cabin?"

"Exactly," Fernando said. "So I'm thinking the Foreman might be camping somewhere up there. When I flushed him out of Three Hills Ranch, he was carrying bedding and other supplies to his white car."

Again Jodie didn't respond.

"I mean, what other leads do we have?" Fernando asked.

"Okay...well, maybe I'll pay bear claw man another visit," she said and clicked off.

Now what? He knew Estelle was pissed and would pitch a fit when she arrived, so he decided to cook dinner as a way to mitigate her anger. He found a sirloin steak in the refrigerator and decided to make Green Chile Stew. He started by chopping garlic and onion and cubing the sirloin. Then he sautéed the garlic and onion in olive oil. Next he browned the sirloin in the garlic and onions with lots of cumin and oregano and then added green chile and beef broth. Separately he boiled a couple of potatoes, cubed them, and tossed them into the mixture.

Leaving the pot on low burn, he opened a Modelo and sat at the kitchen table drinking the beer. The sound of a car pulling into the driveway startled him, because he didn't expect Estelle until much later. He jumped up from the kitchen table and looked out the window at Estelle's Camry pulling into the garage. A sense of relief calmed him. It wasn't the white ghost.

His relief lasted all of ten seconds. Then Estelle burst through the kitchen door, raising her voice: "What's going on, Fernando? What haven't you told me?"

Estelle stopped and sniffed, smelling the green chile stew. "What's cooking?"

"Green chile stew," Fernando said. "I thought you might like it."

"I do, but I still want to know what's going on," Estelle said, staring at him. She wasn't going to let him off the hook that easily.

Fernando pointed to the kitchen table. Estelle sat across from him. Hoping for the best, Fernando reminded her about busting the Foreman at Three Hills Ranch and explained that the Foreman had come back to get even with those who sent him to prison, namely Fernando and Antonio and a Santa Fe County Sheriff named Jodie Williams. Then he recounted the entire series of events since the Foreman arrived in town, beginning with the murder of two Santa Fe cops. He told Estelle about the attempts on his and Antonio's lives. And he told her about the murder of Richard Clark and the attempted murder of his wife, Joan Clark. He left out the bear claw man because by that time his tale of woe had become too complicated. He finally threw up his hands and said, "In short, there's a cop killer in town who's trying to kill the three of us, Antonio and Jodie and me."

Estelle shook her head, disgusted. "I don't understand. You're supposed to be retired. How do you keep getting involved in these things?"

"I know, I know, but I didn't choose to get involved with this," Fernando pleaded. "This Three Hills Ranch case just keeps coming back from the dead to haunt us."

Estelle sighed. "So what are we going to do?"

"I think you should pack a bag and go stay with Flavia and Luis for a couple of days, just until this situation resolves. It shouldn't take too long, I promise," Fernando said, regretting his promise as soon as he made it. But he figured Estelle would be safe in Tesuque with their daughter and her husband, high profile lawyers who lived in a big house overlooking the Santa Fe Opera.

"Oh, Fernando, what have you done...?" Estelle clucked her tongue. "Okay, I'll pack a bag after dinner and go stay with Flavia."

"Good," Fernando said.

Estelle pointed her finger at him. "But this is your problem. You fix it!"

11

The sound of a car on Acequia Madre Street woke Fernando in the middle of the night. Half asleep, he flailed around in his bed, feeling the empty space where his wife always slept. He was confused for a moment. Then he remembered. Estelle had gone to stay with Flavia and Luis for a few days. His nerves were on edge, hair trigger. He had a hard enough time sleeping without Estelle; he didn't need this turmoil with the Foreman. Out of desperation he closed his eyes and tried to will himself to sleep. He dozed off intermittently but woke at the slightest sound.

Sometime near dawn, with the eastern sky just beginning to lighten, he awoke when another car came racing down the street and skidded into his driveway. His mind cleared the moment he heard the car honk. A split second later he heard a muffled Thok! Thok! Thok! from outside followed by his kitchen windows shattering. The moment he dreaded had arrived. It was show time.

Fernando jumped out of bed and pulled on a pair of jeans under his oversized T-shirt. He quickly pulled on his boots, grabbed his Smith & Wesson, and headed for the old front door they hadn't used in years. The security alarm went off when he unlatched and forced open the door, but he let the siren blast hoping it would drive away the shooter before he could damage the house any further.

Outside the fresh air gave him the energy he needed. He crouched low and moved steadily through the bushes and the cottonwoods toward the gunfire. In the half-light of dawn he could make out the outline of a car straight ahead and two shadowy figures nearby. The Foreman stood in front of the car carrying a semi-automatic rifle. Looked like an AR-14. The other man, closest to Fernando, held only a handgun. Fernando recognized him by his clothing: jeans and a white T-shirt. It was none other than the Foreman's accomplice at Three Hills Ranch where he'd seen them loading supplies into the white Audi.

The two shooters stood frozen, watching his kitchen door. No doubt they were waiting for Fernando to come blazing out of the door where they could mow him down, like the old Butch Cassidy and Sundance Kid movie. Not a bad plan, except that he had an alternative exit on the other side of the house. And he was smart enough to use it. Now Fernando had the advantage of surprise.

While the Foreman stared at the kitchen door waiting, Fernando crept closer. He stayed in the shadows as much as possible, hiding behind a row of bushes lining the street. His plan was simple. He would flank the two shooters and order them to drop their weapons. It might have worked had he not stumbled on a half-buried tree root. The sound alerted the man in the white T-shirt, who turned and yelled. A split second later the man opened fire with his pistol: Pop! Pop! The bullets tore through the bushes, shredding the leaves and branches above Fernando.

Fernando had no choice. He pointed his Smith & Wesson and pulled the trigger: Pop! The bullet struck the gunman in his upper chest and sent him staggering backwards. Holding his chest, the gunman crumpled to the ground. The Foreman shouted something to his companion and then turned to look for Fernando, who crouched below the bushes, out of sight.

"Show yourself!" the Foreman bellowed. "Or I'll go into the house and kill everyone I find there."

Fernando answered by peeking over the top of the bushes and firing wildly: Pop! Pop! Then he dove onto the ground and lay flat.

The Foreman cursed and sprayed the bushes with his weapon: Thok! Thok! Thok! Thok!

Fernando hugged the ground. He didn't dare get to his feet. If he stood he was a dead man. Instead, he would wait until the Foreman came closer and then shoot the sonofabitch through the bushes. As soon as he had a clear shot, he would empty his Smith & Wesson.

But the Foreman wasn't stupid. He paused, deciding what to do. A siren off in the distance made the decision for him. A police car was on its way, responding to Fernando's home security alarm.

The Foreman ran to his car and climbed inside, not bothering with the man in the white T-shirt. He didn't even look at his fallen companion. He backed out of the driveway and then shot off fast up Acequia Madre, away from the approaching police car.

Fernando stood up and watched the white ghost disappear down Delgado Street. The Foreman would make his way to East Alameda and then down to the Paseo. From there he would be out of the city in a few minutes, on his way to wherever he was hiding out.

Once the Foreman was gone, Fernando climbed through the bushes to where the man in the white T-shirt lay. The gunman lay on his back with his eyes open and a gaping wound in his chest. A dark red stain had spread over the front of the man's white T-shirt. Fernando knelt on the gravel driveway and tried to find a pulse. He gave up after a few seconds.

In the half-light of dawn Fernando didn't recognize the dead man as one of Warner's men at Three Hills Ranch. Must be someone new who the Foreman had recruited, he decided. Maybe someone the Foreman had met in prison.

Just then the siren came screaming up Acequia Madre and turned into his driveway. Fernando raised his hand to greet the officer, a former colleague from his years on the Santa Fe Police Department.

Paul Romero jumped out of his cruiser and walked up to Fernando. "Home invasion?"

"Yeah," Fernando said, pointing to his kitchen windows. "Two of them. One got away, this one didn't."

"Do you know who they were?" Paul asked.

"Yeah, one was Carter Hoover, better known as the Foreman," Fernando said. "Manny and Antonio can fill you in on this guy. He's the shooter who killed Sean Beatty and Matt Medina."

"Shit...you're a lucky man."

Fernando frowned. "I don't feel so damn lucky."

Paul walked over and knelt beside the dead man. He gingerly removed the man's wallet and examined the contents. "Steve Bivins, age forty-seven, from Socorro. Sound familiar?"

"Never heard of him," Fernando said.

Paul nodded. "Okay. They'll run a check on him at the station."

With that, Paul called the station and told them to hold the ambulance and send Forensics instead. While they waited for Forensics, Fernando gave his statement to Paul, but only the basics. He didn't want to get bogged down in a longwinded narrative about what happened at Three Hills Ranch years ago. Better to stick to this one incident, at least for the time being.

As soon as Forensics arrived Fernando walked back to the house. The entire front bank of windows had been shattered. Inside the kitchen he saw several bullet holes in the rear wall and kitchen cabinets. Wait until Estelle sees this, he kept thinking. He was already in the doghouse.

He took a deep breath and told himself to take it one step at a time. That was the only way to handle the situation. Don't think, just act. First, he swept up all the glass on the kitchen floor, including the fragments of glass remaining in the sill that he knocked out with a rubber hammer.

Next he went to the garage and brought back his staple gun and a sheet of clear plastic he used as a painting drop cloth. He stapled the plastic over the open windows and then called Dick Murphy and ordered replacement glass for the windows. Then he spackled the bullet holes in the wall and kitchen cabinets. After the spackle dried, he would sand and touch up the area with paint he kept in the garage. By the day after tomorrow, with a little luck, the kitchen would be as good as new. Estelle might not notice the damage. If she did notice, he would tell he wanted to surprise her with new kitchen windows. Most of the windows in their house were at least twenty years old.

Finished, he opened a Modelo and sat at the kitchen table brooding. He doubted the Foreman would return, given the reception he'd received. But that didn't solve a damned thing. They needed to find the Foreman's lair and either capture or lay him out like the man with the white T-shirt. At this point Fernando didn't care which. Just as long as he was gone.

12

Dick Murphy's panel truck pulled into Fernando's driveway a few minutes after Noon. Fernando watched from his kitchen door as the tall gangly old geezer eased out of his truck and stretched his back. With his scraggly gray stubble and skin the color of burnt bacon, Dick was the picture of someone who'd aged badly. He wore his usual baseball cap and blue work shirt with the Dick's Door and Window logo. Despite his appearance, Dick's Door and Window service had been the best in town for over forty years.

Coughing and wheezing, Dick ambled through the garden and up to the kitchen door. He stopped to look at the bank of missing windows and frowned. "What the hell happened here?" he asked, looking through the paint-splattered plastic sheet stapled over the windows.

"Night visitors," Fernando said. "They weren't very friendly."

"Hmmm..." Dick said, running his hand under the plastic and over the empty window frames. He took a yellow and black DeWalt tape measure off a hook on his jeans and measured the two identical windows that together formed the window bank. "Hmmm..." he repeated.

Fernando waited while Dick stroked his stubbled chin.

"Tell you what, Fernando," Dick said. "Both these frames are damaged, pretty much beyond repair. You'd be better off replacing the two windows, frames and all. They're a standard size, so I could pick up a couple from Home Depot and pop 'em in this afternoon. You'd have to paint the frames, but that would be the easiest way to repair the damage."

"Fine," Fernando said. "But I need it fixed quick before Estelle returns. She sees this, she'll have a fit."

"She go on vacation?" Dick asked.

Fernando shook his head. "No, I sent her to stay with Flavia for a couple of days to avoid this. I had a warning these guys were going to show up."

Dick looked at him funny. "Why, is someone after you or something?"

"That's the long and short of it, yes," Fernando said.

Dick nodded. "Okay, I'll pick up the windows and be back this afternoon. If you leave, just put a key under the doormat. Shouldn't take more'n a couple hours to drop 'em in."

After Dick left, Fernando made himself a sandwich for lunch and sat at the kitchen table, trying to avoid looking at the paint-splattered plastic sheet over his empty windows. Ugly as sin. If Dick replaced the windows this afternoon, he could paint the interior and exterior frames this evening and be off the hook when Estelle returned tomorrow or the next day. Then he remembered the bullet holes in the wall and the cabinets that he'd spackled. He would still have to sand and paint them to match the white wall and the blue cabinets, which would take more time, probably run in to tomorrow morning. Given the work required of him, his plan was to hang around the house all day and help Dick, if Dick needed an assistant. The most important thing was to get the windows in as quickly as possible.

His plan changed when his cell phone rang. He tensed when he saw Jodie's name on the screen.

"Hey, Fernando, I'm just getting back to you now," Jodie said. "We had a shooting out in Nambé that's tied me up."

"Nambé? I thought only rich people lived in Nambé."

Jodie laughed. "Yeah, but the rich shoot people too."

"If you say so," Fernando said.

"Anyway, I'm just now getting ready to go back to the Shaggy Peak Trail," Jodie said. "I want to ask bear claw man if it's true he knows where the Foreman's hiding. Are you game?"

Fernando looked around at the missing windows and the patches of spackle that needed sanding and painting. He knew he shouldn't, but he did anyway. "I'm game. How soon will you be at the trail?"

"I'm leaving now. I'll be there in fifteen minutes," Jodie said.

Before leaving, Fernando grabbed a bottle of water out of the refrigerator and reloaded his Smith & Wesson. He almost forgot to leave a key for Dick. He had to back up and climb out of the Cherokee and walk back to the kitchen door. He took the house key off his key chain and placed it under their 'Welcome' doormat, just as Dick instructed. He only hoped Dick remembered to put it back because it was his only key to the house.

Then he retraced his route to the Shaggy Peak Trail. Once out of town on the Old Las Vegas Highway he buzzed down the front windows of the Cherokee and let the cool breeze blow over him. It was his favorite time of year, with the summer temps cooling and the mesas ablaze with yellow chamisa and white and purple wildflowers. He could smell the sage and the rosemary and the other vegetation, not a whiff of humidity in the dry air.

As always, Jodie had arrived first. She was standing by her cruiser at the trailhead as Fernando pulled into the parking lot. He parked next to a red Volvo, a $70,000 electric automobile. Good old Santa Fe. Even hikers rode around in expensive electric cars. Shaking his head, he left his bottle of water in the cup holder and locked up the Cherokee.

Fernando waited for Jodie to deliver her usual line.

Jodie didn't disappoint him. "What took you so long?"

"Traffic," Fernando said.

Jodie nodded and then took off up the trail with Fernando following. He simply could not keep up with the woman.

"Hey—wait for me," Fernando said.

Jodie stopped, waiting for Fernando to catch up. While they walked, Fernando told her about his early morning visitors, the Foreman and an accomplice named Steve Bivins.

"Who's Steve Bivins?" Jodie asked.

Fernando shook his head. "He's the dead man. That's all I know."

Halfway up to the cabin they spotted a black bear cub alongside the trail. The cub took one look at them and hightailed it back into the forest. Fernando stopped, looking around for the momma bear. Bears could be especially ferocious if they thought their cubs were in danger.

Jodie also stopped. "Do you see momma?"

"No, looks like the cub's old enough to fend for itself," Fernando said.

They continued hiking up the trail. Just before the place where Joan Clark had fallen, still marked off by yellow caution tape, they cut over to the forest road with the bear signs nailed to trees. The cabin slowly came into view through the tall ponderosa pines. No sign of bear claw man or anyone else. They approached cautiously, noticing the ax was missing from the tree stump in front of the cabin. Which meant bear claw man was armed and maybe dangerous.

"We don't want to surprise him," Fernando said. "He didn't look like the most stable of individuals."

Jodie gave him a funny look.

"Anyone home?" Fernando shouted, walking up to the door.

When no one responded, Fernando swung the door open and looked into the one-room cabin. Again there was no sign of bear claw man or his ax. The place looked exactly the same as it did on their last visit, except the first-aid bandages on the table had been cleared away.

Jodie stood back from the door, hands on her hips. She scanned the surrounding forest, which seemed to deepen as it climbed the mountain. Finally she walked around behind the cabin and stood staring at a thick patch of gnarly juniper trees and tangled wild rose and sumac bushes on a slight rise about fifty yards up the mountain. A thin ribbon of a path led up to the rise.

Fernando came around back to join her. “What do you see?”

Jodie pointed toward the hill. “I thought I saw movement in that overgrowth. As if someone was watching us.”

Fernando didn’t see anything but nodded anyway.

“Let’s check it out,” Jodie said, leading the way.

Fernando followed Jodie up the rise. Now he saw it too, the bushes shaking from something moving inside. Maybe it was a wild animal. “Careful, it might be the mother bear,” Fernando warned.

That gave Jodie pause. Then she shook her head. “I don’t think so, we’ve gone too far.”

Fernando had his hand on his Smith & Wesson as they approached the rise. Just in case.

Suddenly a furry object poked its head out of the bushes.

Both Fernando and Jodie jumped back, but it was only bear claw man’s head poking out. “Go away!” he barked. “Get away from here while you still can. Before they see you!”

Fernando and Jodie stared at bear claw man, who squatted on all fours like a real bear with his head sticking out of the bushes.

Jodie spoke first. “Sir, we need to ask you a few more questions. Questions about those men who pushed the woman off the cliff and murdered her husband.”

“And by the way, thanks for rescuing the woman,” Fernando added, trying to ease tensions. “We understand you helped her, even bandaged her wounds. She told us she was very grateful for your help.”

Hearing that, bear claw man crawled out of the bushes with his axe. He sat up and put the axe down. He watched them approach. “I warned you before. I told you to stay away.”

Jodie tried again. “Joan Clark, the woman you saved, told us you’d seen the two men who killed her husband before and knew where they were staying. We need to stop them from killing again.”

Bear claw man started twisting and turning his head this way and that. “I can’t talk. You don’t understand. You need to get out of here before they see you. You’re in danger.”

Fernando ignored the warning and persisted. “You said you knew where these men were staying. Can you tell us where?”

“In the woods,” bear claw man said, motioning toward the east, where one forested ridge after another receded into the Pecos Wilderness.

"Okay, but where in the woods?" Fernando asked.

"I told you, I can't talk," Bear Claw Man said. "Leave me alone! Go away before the bears get you!"

"Wait," Jodie said. "Are they camping in the forest? Can you at least tell us that much?"

Without answering, bear claw man crawled back into the bushes and disappeared from view.

"Sir, you're the only person who can tell us where to find these people," Jodie repeated. "Will you help us?"

Bear claw man did not respond. Moments later his arm reached out and grabbed the axe, pulling it back into the bushes.

Fernando and Jodie spent a few more minutes trying to convince bear claw man to talk, but he refused to come out or speak to them.

Finally Jodie gave up. She shrugged and started walking back to the trail. When Fernando joined her, she turned and asked, "Do you think he's nuts...or is he speaking about bears metaphorically?"

"Damned if I know," Fernando said.

13

After Jodie drove off, Fernando sat in the Cherokee for a few minutes brooding, as was his habit. He doubted they'd ever get any more information about the Foreman from bear claw man, who seemed not only intimidated but scared to death of the Foreman. So where did that leave them? He had no idea where the Foreman was hiding out. Bear claw man's "in the woods" could mean anything–plus, the man was hardly a reliable source. The one place Fernando knew for certain the Foreman had been sighted was Three Hills Ranch. Since he was already halfway to the ranch, he decided to continue on down to Three Hills. This time he would drive into the ranch and have a look around, not just observe from the top of the hill.

So he turned right on the Old Las Vegas Highway and drove down to the Highway 285 exchange and quickly turned south on Highway 41 toward the village of Galisteo. He remembered the road to Three Hills Ranch started in an arroyo bed just before the bridge over Galisteo Creek. He slowed down as he approached the bridge, looking for the arroyo. What he saw surprised him. The usually dry arroyo had a trickle of water meandering down the center of the arroyo toward the bridge. The wet sand might be a problem for the Cherokee. Time to rethink.

Stopping on the side of the highway, Fernando looked for another route to the ranch. No road, but he saw tire tracks on the mesa, where more than one vehicle had jumped the ditch and driven a winding path through a field of sage and chamisa. So he fired up the Cherokee and bounced over the ditch, following the tracks as they zig-zagged across the mesa toward the three hills that surrounded the ranch and gave it its name. Halfway there he found the remnants of the dirt road where it came up from the arroyo. From there it was an easy drive to the entrance of Three Hills Ranch, located between two massive outcroppings of rock.

He drove through the rock outcroppings and pulled up at the guard station, a tiny wooden building not much bigger than an old fashioned outhouse. Empty, its door wide open. This, he remembered, was where the Foreman or one of Warner's other hired hands monitored who came and went at Three Hills Ranch. Virtually no one entered or exited the ranch who wasn't first cleared by the Foreman.

Warner and his network of human traffickers brought in young women from border towns like Juarez and Nogales. The young women, some of them underage, were held captive at the ranch and offered as sex slaves to the rich men who Warner flew to the ranch from the Santa Fe and Albuquerque airports. A few of the young women tried to escape, including some who went over the hill to the highway on the trail he'd taken last time he'd come. Most of those who made it over the hill died on the highway. Murdered by Warner's posses before they could hitch a ride and reach the safety of Santa Fe. Full of bad memories, this place. As Ester Hoke said, it was a place where evil things had happened, including the murder of her husband.

Fernando jumped out of the Cherokee and looked around the empty yard. The white ghost was nowhere to be seen. He walked around to the back hatch and grabbed his Steyr, then had a change of heart. The Steyr wouldn't be good in close quarters. So with his Smith & Wesson in hand, he walked directly up the drive toward the square, fortress-like mansion built around a central courtyard. He walked on by the mansion, deciding to first search the barracks where he'd first seen the late Steve Bivins, the man wearing the white T-shirt that he'd shot back at his house on Acequia Madre. Then he would attend to the mansion.

Fernando climbed the steps to the porch and then marched into the elongated wooden barracks. Inside he saw the familiar dormitory style interior divided by half-walls into ten bedrooms or living units, each with a bed, bureau, and sitting chair. Walking down the corridor he found most of the beds with sheets and blankets either missing or tossed on the floor. At the end of the corridor he came to the open bathroom containing sinks, showers, and toilet stalls. It looked like the facilities had been used recently, because soiled paper towels and toilet paper were scattered over the floor and the long counter. Two of the toilets and one of the sinks were clogged and backed up. He figured vagrants of one kind or another had been here and left the mess.

Fernando checked each of the ten units but found nothing other than scattered bedclothes. No one really knew how many young women had been imprisoned here, drugged and beaten and forced to have sex with the wealthy men who came to the ranch to have sex with anonymous, underage girls without having to worry about consequences, legal or otherwise. They were swine, human predators.

Turning away in disgust, Fernando marched quickly out of the barracks and walked back toward the mansion. On the way he spied Warner's helipad off to the right. He hesitated for a moment, not sure he wanted to revisit the sight of Warner's death. Finally out of curiosity he climbed slowly up the steps to the helipad. What he saw shocked him. The blackened concrete pad still reeked of the smell of the fireball that had consumed the hillside and melted much of Warner's helicopter. Standing on the greasy blackened helipad he had a flashback of Warner's fiery death. He saw in his mind's eye what he usually saw only in the nightmares that had plagued him ever since that day five years ago:

Jodie shouted at them from the trail leading to the helipad. She pointed toward the helicopter pad. "He's escaping! He's up here!" she shouted.

Jodie ran toward the helicopter pad, while he and Antonio lagged behind. They ran up the hill to where the trail to the tea-house veered to the left and circled around behind the house to the helipad. From about fifty yards away they could see that Warner had already reached the copter and was attempting to start the engine, the blades beginning to churn.

Jodie reached the stairway up to the helipad just as the copter began to lift off. She took out her service revolver and waved it at Warner, ordering him to stop. Suddenly she was engulfed in a windstorm that churned up dust and dead brush from the hillside. Partially blinded, she shot at the helicopter once and then again, hearing the ping of the bullets striking the metal.

She kept firing, blinded by the dust, until she had to turn away and cover her face with her arm.

Lifting off, Warner took his eyes off the instrument panel for just an instant and looked down at Jodie. In that instant the copter rolled to the right, its blades just grazing the side of the hill behind the pad. The copter spun out of control. It somersaulted grotesquely and then crashed into the hillside, bursting into flames. Suddenly the machine exploded, sending fragments hurtling through the air and then when they reached their zenith slowly falling to the ground in slow motion. The fragments, some flaming and some burned black, showered the area with twisted, smoking metal that stank of burning fuel and electronics.

Jodie stumbled back down the hill, coughing from the acrid smell. "Get back! The smoke is toxic!" she shouted at them. She bent over, hands on her knees, struggling for air.

They waited for her at the bottom of the hill until she finally came weaving down the trail coughing. From a distance the three of them watched the fragments flame and then burn out on the hillside.

Fernando turned, as if turning his back on the memory, and walked quickly down the stairway in order to escape the image that still haunted him. Walk away quickly, focus on each step you take and don't think. Stay in motion, do something, that had become his way of coping with the bad memories that had piled up over the years and more than once had threatened to pull him down into clinical depression. Once, after an especially gruesome murder in Santa Fe, his family doc had prescribed an anti-depressant. He took the meds for about a week before he threw them away because the damn pills made his brain fuzzy and his body feel like cement. He started exercising instead, which he did for a couple of weeks before saying the hell with that too. Since then he'd simply told himself to suck it up whenever he started feeling depressed. Who didn't feel depressed these days?

Once down the stairway, he walked across the yard to the mansion. Most of the lush plantings along the empty water canal that surrounded the front of the mansion had died, leaving a yellow and brown tangle of dead flowers and shrubs. As dry as bales of straw. Coming closer, he noticed the Territorial style windows were all shuttered tight. The front door, on the other hand, jutted open. Looked to Fernando like someone had broken in and left the door open.

Fernando approached the door cautiously with his Smith & Wesson in his right hand. He moved the front door open with his left foot and ducked behind the jam. Inside the front anteroom looked deserted. Then he saw the refuse littering the floor and furniture: food wrappers, empty bottles and cans, used clothing and other trash left behind by vandals or vagrants. He smiled at the irony. From a millionaire's sex ranch to a vagrant's hideout, quite a downfall.

He moved cautiously through the anteroom. He noticed the dry fountain in the center courtyard now surrounded by dead flowerbeds. Like the shrubbery outside, the flowerbeds had shriveled to an ugly brown color. Staying to the left, he entered the east wing of the mansion toward the kitchen and dining areas, if he remembered correctly. Halfway there he heard a noise from one of the rooms further down the hall. Sounded like a heavy object dropping, maybe a suitcase or backpack. Someone else was in the mansion. The Foreman? Or maybe the ghost of Robert Warner himself, come back to haunt what remained of his evil empire.

"Who's there?" Fernando called out, readying his Smith & Wesson.

Suddenly a blur came running down the hallway toward him, a

young girl dressed in a dirty Nike T-shirt and black tights. He managed to tuck his Smith & Wesson in its holster before she collided with him. She yelped and grabbed him around the waist as they fell. He turned to his side to avoid landing on the child. Grabbing the girl's arm, he caught a good look at her dirty little face and matted black hair. Maybe nine or ten years old, max.

"Hey, little girl, where are your parents?" Fernando asked, struggling to get to his feet.

The girl fought against him, trying to free her arm. "*Por favor*."

Just then a man and a woman who he took to be the girl's parents came running down the hallway. The mother grabbed the young girl and held her in her arms. "*Gracias, señor*," she said to Fernando, a tiny woman with round face, bronze skin, and short black hair. She looked to be in her late twenties, early thirties. She wore jeans and a thin blue sweater over a T-shirt.

"Where are you headed?" Fernando asked.

The woman shook her head. "*No habla inglés*."

The father stepped forward, a short muscular man wearing jeans and a dark green hoodie. "*Vamos a Denver*."

"Family?" Fernando asked.

"*Si, la familia*," the man said, nodding his head.

While the mother held the little girl, the father told Fernando their story. They were from a small village south of Juarez controlled by the Sinaloa Cartel. The cartel had murdered the wife's brother, who lived with them, and burned down their house. They took whatever possessions they were able to save and paid a syndicate to get them across the border. They'd been walking and hitching rides for the last two days. Their last ride had been a rancher from Galisteo. He told them about this place and dropped them off last night. But they were hungry now and wanted to leave, maybe go to Santa Fe to find food and water before continuing on to Denver. They hoped to find a church or an organization that would help them find a ride to Denver.

Fernando raised his hand to speak. He took a card out of his wallet and handed it to the father, whose name was Tomas. Printed in both Spanish and English, the card advertised Estelle's organization, the Saint Francis Immigrant Outreach Program. "*Mi esposa*," he said, pointing to the card.

Fernando explained that the Outreach Program would help them with food and clothing and temporary shelter on their way to Denver.

Tomas smiled. "*Gracias, señor*!"

Fernando waited while the mother and father went down the hall to get their belongings. The little girl stayed with him, her big gray eyes staring at him from across the hallway. She smiled when she saw her parents returning, dragging their bulky canvas backpacks behind them.

Fernando led them outside to the Cherokee and opened the doors for them. He placed their backpacks in the rear hatch and hid the Steyr in the hidden compartment below the mat so as not to frighten them.

Tomas sat in the front seat while his wife and their daughter sat in the back.

On the way to Santa Fe Fernando told them a bit about Santa Fe, how it was an ancient city founded in 1610 by Spanish pilgrims and soldiers traveling up the El Camino Real from Mexico City. Tomas nodded, seeming to understand. Tomas probably knew as much about the El Camino Real as Fernando did.

When they reached Santa Fe, Fernando drove directly to the Immigrant Outreach office directly behind the Cathedral Basilica of Saint Francis. He helped Tomas unload the heavy backpacks and carry them into the office, where Estelle and two other women were sorting clothing on large tables in the back room.

Estelle came right over to help the family.

"I found them hiding at Three Hills Ranch," Fernando said.

Estelle nodded. "Good. I'm glad you brought them in."

As Fernando was leaving Tomas came up to him and shook his hand. "Thank you," he said.

Fernando waved and turned to walk out of the office. As he stepped through the door he happened to notice Estelle smiling at him. She pointed him out and said something about him to the family.

Fernando smiled back, proud to have done something that met Estelle's approval. For a change.

14

Fernando tossed and turned most of the night, buffeted by nightmares of his encounters with the Foreman. He awoke in a cold sweat, made even worse when he realized Estelle was missing from his bed. He felt abandoned, even though it was his idea that Estelle stay with Flavia for a couple of days. He comforted himself with the knowledge that she would return home this evening. Funny how he'd become so dependent on Estelle for his peace of mind. They'd been together so long that when she was gone it felt like a part of him was missing. Damn, he was getting sentimental in his old age.

He climbed out of bed and staggered into the kitchen to make himself a cup of coffee. Coffee before anything else, that was his routine. He needed to stick to his routines, especially with Estelle absent. After brewing himself a cup in the Keurig, he took the cup into his study and brooded. He couldn't get the Foreman out of his mind. The bastard had tried to kill both him and Antonio, which meant Jodie might be next. He hoped Jodie took the threat seriously. She didn't seem that worried when he told her about the Foreman's reappearance in Santa Fe.

The coffee cleared his head, so he made another cup and ate a quick breakfast of oatmeal with fruit because he was too lazy to cook eggs. Then he showered and dressed, always trying to avoid looking in the mirror. He refused to own the image he saw staring back at him in the mirror, the gray hair and the wrinkled face. Estelle laughed at his refusal to look in the mirror as if it was some kind of joke. But it was no joke. Not to him, anyway.

Before leaving, he finished sanding and painting the patched kitchen walls and cabinets. Then he put the Steyr back in his office closet. He decided to rely on the Smith & Wesson today because of its mobility. He had no idea what the day would bring. The hall clock chimed ten o'clock as he left the house, making sure to set the security alarm and lock the door. He climbed in the Cherokee and drove to the Paseo and around to Marcy Street, where he turned left and pulled into the parking lot of the Washington Avenue Station. Before anything else, he wanted to update Antonio on yesterday's events.

Fernando parked in a visitor's space and walked through the front door. The day dispatcher sat behind the counter. She smiled when she saw him. "You know, I just had a hunch you'd show up today, what with all the talk about this Foreman guy. Plus, I know how much you miss us. I'm surprised you aren't in the Chief's office right now asking for your job back!"

"Hah!" Fernando said, laughing. He loved Linda's sense of humor. An old hippie with long gray hair and a wicked sense of humor, she'd moved down to Santa Fe from Taos in the late 1970s after becoming disillusioned with living in the New Buffalo commune. He'd had a brief affair with Linda many years ago, his only indiscretion in the forty years he'd been married to Estelle. They'd broken it off to save their friendship... as well as his marriage.

"Oh, come on, fess up, you miss us," Linda said.

Fernando nodded. "Some of you, it's true. Then there's the Chief."

Linda smiled. "He misses you too."

"I can imagine. I was his whipping boy for years."

"So what's up?" Linda asked.

"I need to talk to Antonio," Fernando said. "I had another pleasant encounter with the Foreman."

"He's back there somewhere," Linda said, pointing down the hall just as her phone rang.

Fernando waved and proceeded down the hall. He found Antonio in the Break Room, drinking a cup of coffee. The big man hunched over the table reading the day's *Independent* with a scowl on his face. He looked up when he saw Fernando enter the room, outfitted with one long table and several chairs, with a coffee maker and refrigerator on a countertop along one wall. The room smelled old and musty, like too many tired bodies had rested there and consumed too much bad food. Welcome to the Washington Avenue Station.

"I've got some news," Fernando said, pulling a chair up to the table.

"Me too," Antonio said. "You go first."

"The Foreman showed up at my house yesterday morning," Fernando said. "He brought another guy with him by the name of Steve Bivins, from Socorro. We think Bivins may have been in the Big House with the Foreman. They shot up my house, busted out the kitchen windows and would have killed me if I hadn't gone out the back door and flanked them. I shot and killed Bivins, but the Foreman got away, driving that white

Audi."

Antonio frowned. "Too bad it wasn't the Foreman. Be rid of him once and for all."

"So what's your news?" Fernando asked.

Antonio sighed. "Yesterday the sonofabitch tried to follow me home again. My shift ended at three o'clock. He must have known that, because he was waiting for me somewhere off the Paseo, maybe in the big parking lot by the Statehouse. I noticed him behind me on Old Santa Fe Trail halfway to the interstate. I knew it was him when I saw that goddamn white car."

"So you didn't get the license number?" Fernando asked.

"No, because the state of New Mexico in all its wisdom doesn't require a front license plate," Antonio said.

Fernando nodded his agreement.

"No way I was gonna show him where I live," Antonio continued. "I'm unlisted for a reason–I like to be off grid. I get my mail at a post office box in Pecos, where nobody knows me. Just the way I like it."

"So what did you do?" Fernando asked.

"I took him to the one place he didn't want to be," Antonio said, laughing. "I swerved onto Twenty-five South and drove like a motherfucker to Cerrillos Road and back down to the police substation on Camino Entrada. Then I quick bailed out of my Jeep and waited behind it with my weapon in hand, just in case he was stupid enough to come after me. But he wasn't. Soon as he saw where I was, he sped off on Cerrillos Road into the city."

"Good thinking," Fernando said.

"Yeah, I suppose, but the thing is, he'll be back," Antonio said. "We need a plan of action, now. The longer we wait, the more we're in danger."

"I wonder. Maybe we can use his persistence to our advantage," Fernando said, thinking of a plan.

"How's that?"

"What if we set him up? You think he'll follow you again today?" Fernando asked.

Antonio shrugged. "Maybe."

"Okay then, let's give it a shot," Fernando said. "How about this? What if I wait at the Bobcat Bite parking lot, and when you and the Foreman drive by, I follow? That way I could come in behind him in your driveway and block him, trap him between us. Two against one. I like those odds, even if he has an assault rifle."

Antonio thought for a moment. "I suppose, but if you don't make it, or even if you're late, I could be in deep shit. There has to be no possibility of a fuck-up. Absolutely none."

"What's the alternative?" Fernando asked. "We're just waiting for him to show up at our doors. He's bound to find out where you live sooner or later. If we don't call the shots, he will."

Antonio sighed. "Then let's do it today. My shift changes tomorrow."

"Okay," Fernando said. "If your shift ends at three, you should be driving by Bobcat Bite around three thirty, right? So I'll make sure to be there a few minutes before three."

Antonio frowned. "And in case he doesn't show up, I'll give you a call. So we're on, unless you hear from me. Okay?"

Fernando nodded. "When he follows you into your driveway, I'll pull in behind him," he said. "No way for him to escape."

"Just remember," Antonio said, staring at Fernando. "No fuck-ups."

15

As the time to leave drew near Fernando began to feel nervous. What could go wrong usually did go wrong in his line of work. This plan was his idea. It would be on him if it backfired.

He waited impatiently until two thirty and then locked his office and headed out. He stopped first at his house on Acequia Madre to pick up the Steyr. For this encounter he might need extra firepower, so he loaded the rifle and placed it between the two front seats for easy access. Then he drove around the Paseo to Old Santa Fe Trail and the Old Las Vegas Highway. When he came to Bobcat Bite he parked in one of the spaces close to the entrance, where he could get back on the highway fast. Only a couple of cars occupied the parking lot, people enjoying a late lunch or an early drink, he figured. Better to keep a low profile. He didn't want to have to explain his presence here at this odd hour. If someone asked, he would say he was waiting for a friend. Which was the truth. Sort of.

Time check: two fifty-five.

While he waited, he checked his Smith & Wesson to make sure it was fully loaded. He always carried an extra box of 41 Magnum ammo in his glove compartment, just in case. Satisfied, he placed his weapon in its holster.

Time check: three ten.

Antonio would have called by now if the Foreman hadn't shown up. Their plan was a go.

Fernando stepped out of his Cherokee and walked around behind the hatch. From here he could observe the highway without being seen. The highway was quiet, too quiet for comfort. Without traffic, the Cherokee would be the only vehicle following the white ghost. That meant he would have to lay back a considerable distance so as not to be conspicuous. Fernando shook his head, trying to stop thinking about all the things that could go wrong.

Time check: three thirty.

Why were they so late? Had something unexpected happened? He began to worry for real now. Antonio always left the station quickly, eager to get back to his cabin in the National Forest. He took out his cell phone to call Antonio.

Just then Fernando heard a vehicle coming over the hill from Santa Fe. He watched as Antonio's orange Jeep Wrangler came slowly over the rise and down the hill. Moments later the white ghost shimmered over the rise, a white blur reflecting the afternoon sunlight.

Fernando put his cell phone back in his pocket and waited.

As soon as the two vehicles passed by, he jumped into the Cherokee and pulled out on the highway. By this time he'd lost sight of both vehicles. That didn't bother him because he knew where Antonio lived. Soon he drove past the tiny village of Glorieta and looked for the forest road that headed north toward La Cueva, an even smaller village. The driveway to Antonio's cabin was off this forest road, about a hundred yards north of the highway.

Moments later he spotted the forest road up ahead. When he turned left onto the road he caught a glimpse of the white ghost disappearing over a small hill. He followed, increasing his speed. He didn't want to leave Antonio alone with the Foreman more than a few seconds.

Topping the hill, Fernando saw Antonio's long driveway below on the left. The Wrangler was halfway down the drive to Antonio's cabin, leaving a trail of dust as it careened over the unmaintained dirt drive.

That's when Fernando's plan went awry. Instead of turning into the drive and following Antonio, the white ghost continued on down the forest road toward La Cueva. Why?

Had the Foreman seen enough for today? Now that he knew where Antonio lived, he could come back at any hour, day or night, to do his dirty work. How else to explain it?

Fernando stopped the Cherokee after turning left into Antonio's drive. He watched the white ghost sail around a long curve and then disappear into the heavy forest that seemed to engulf the road and the Audi. Then he threw the Cherokee in gear and continued on down the drive to Antonio's cabin: a small L-shaped log cabin that Antonio had purchased in Durango as a kit and then assembled by himself. The cabin was built like a fortress, with a steel front door and iron bars over its windows. Antonio was a man who valued his privacy.

The big man stood beside his Wrangler, waiting for Fernando in the clearing beside the cabin.

Fernando parked behind the Wrangler. He checked his rear view mirror to make sure the white ghost wasn't behind him in the drive. It wasn't.

"He didn't follow me," Antonio said, hands on his hips, as Fernando climbed out of the Cherokee.

"I saw," Fernando said, noticing how the surrounding ponderosa pines towered over the cabin and cast shadows across the clearing. He'd never liked Antonio's cabin. Too dark. Too secluded.

"You think he'll come back?" Antonio asked, moving toward the cabin door.

"No idea," Fernando said, distracted. He was looking across the clearing to where the tree-lined hillside rose gradually to a rocky ridge about fifty yards away. "What's up there?"

Antonio shrugged. "La Cueva Canyon. Not much else."

Not knowing the whereabouts of the Foreman made Fernando nervous. The Foreman could be anywhere in the forest. He could be watching them at this very moment.

"I don't like the looks of this," Fernando said.

"Yeah. I think I'll get the rifle outta my Jeep," Antonio said, starting for the Wrangler.

Thok! Thok! Thok! suddenly erupted from the ridge above. The bullets splintered against the cabin and kicked up dust in the clearing.

"Get down!" Fernando shouted.

Instead, Antonio stopped and began firing with his Glock pistol. Pop! Pop!

Thok! Thok! Thok! came the response.

Antonio staggered back and reached for the Jeep. He missed and fell in the dirt holding his abdomen. Moaning, he rolled over on his stomach and held his abdomen tightly.

"Antonio!" Fernando shouted and ran to the big man's side. "Put pressure on the wound. Don't let go. I'll be right back."

Fernando fell down on his hands and knees and crawled to the open door of the Cherokee. He reached in between the front seats and grabbed his Steyr. Using the Cherokee for a shield he poked his rifle over the hood and surveyed the top of the ridge, a scattering of boulders surrounded by trees. Using the scope, he spotted movement off to the left in a stand of new aspen trees, their green and yellow leaves shimmering like glass chimes in the sunlight.

Fernando took aim at a dark shadow behind the leaves and squeezed the trigger. Crack! Then he jacked another round into the chamber of the Steyr and fired again. Crack!

From fifty yards away he heard the Foreman curse angrily, as though he'd been hit. Then the Foreman shouted something that Fernando didn't catch, followed by silence.

Fernando grabbed a jacket he kept in the rear seat of the Cherokee and ran back to Antonio. "Here, hold this against your wound," Fernando said, pushing the jacket under Antonio's stomach.

Antonio moaned as Fernando got back on his feet and called Linda at the Washington Avenue Station. "Linda, it's Fernando. I need you to call Christus Saint Vincent and have them send a medevac. Antonio's badly wounded. We're just off the Old Las Vegas Highway on the road to La Cueva. I'll flag down the helicopter when I see it."

"Okay, but that's gonna take some time," Linda said. "I'll also call for an ambulance in Pecos. They can be there in minutes to stabilize Antonio while you wait for the medevac."

"Good. Thanks," Fernando said and clicked off.

He knelt over Antonio again. "Stay with me, Antonio. The ambulance will be here in a couple of minutes. Come on, buddy. Open your eyes. Don't go to sleep."

Antonio fought to stay awake. His eyes kept closing, but he struggled and opened them again. He continued to moan, holding the now bloody jacket tight against his abdomen.

Just as Fernando heard the siren of an approaching ambulance, he saw the white ghost speed down the road to the highway, leaving billowing dust clouds behind. Had he wounded the Foreman? He'd heard the Foreman cry out, so maybe? Not serious enough to keep him from driving, but serious enough to send him racing back to Santa Fe for medical attention? That was the question.

When the siren grew louder, Fernando placed his Steyr in the Cherokee and ran down the drive waving his arms.

The ambulance driver spotted Fernando and turned into the drive. Stopping, the driver buzzed down the window and asked, "Where's the injured man?"

Gasping for breath, Fernando pointed down toward the cabin.

"Jump in," the driver said, a balding middle-aged man wearing glasses. He waited for Fernando to climb in back and then took off fast down the drive, bouncing over the rough road. The driver pulled up behind the Cherokee. Instantly he bolted out of the ambulance, followed by a younger medic sitting in the passenger's seat carrying a heavy pack. The two medics knelt beside Antonio.

"Sir? Sir? Can you hear me?" the driver asked Antonio, jostling him lightly. "I need you to stay awake, okay? Let me see your wound."

Antonio tried to roll over but it was too painful. He moaned.

The driver had seen enough. He turned to the other medic and yelled, "Start an IV. Quick!"

Fernando felt helpless. He stood back and watched the two medics administer to Antonio. It took them several minutes, but they managed to start an IV and wrap a makeshift bandage around Antonio's midsection. They gave him two injections while they worked. Antonio seemed to relax.

"There's a medevac on its way," Fernando said.

"Good. He's needs to get to an OR as soon as possible," the driver said.

The two medics hovered over Antonio as they waited for the medevac. When they heard the chopper approaching from the west, Fernando walked out in the center of the clearing and waved his arms overhead.

The pilot acknowledged contact by dipping his blades and then slowed down, looking for a flat, safe place to land. He chose a turn-around area in the drive, not far from the clearing in front of the cabin. Descending, the chopper kicked up a mini-tornado of dust and sand and dead grass. The big bird rocked to one side when it touched down and then righted itself, sputtering. The pilot killed the motor, and moments later another medic jumped out of the chopper and rushed over to where Fernando and the others hovered around Antonio.

Fernando let the ambulance medics explain the situation. He walked over by the Cherokee and watched them work. They made sure Antonio was stable before loading him on a stretcher and carrying him and his IV to the chopper. Carrying the six-seven, two hundred and eighty-pound Antonio proved difficult. The big man's feet stuck out over the edge of the stretcher.

When they were ready to take off, the pilot came over to Fernando. "We're going to need some information...can you come with us?" he asked, a small clean-cut young man with a crew-cut, wearing all khaki.

Fernando shook his head. "No, because I have my vehicle here. I'll meet you at Christus Saint Vincent. It shouldn't take me more than twenty or thirty minutes. I'll be right behind you."

The young pilot nodded. "Good enough." Then he ran to join the others in the helicopter.

Fernando watched the medevac lift off, churning up a dust storm as it rose above the trees into the sky. Once aloft, the chopper turned due west and disappeared over the treetops.

Alone now, without knowing the condition of Antonio, Fernando felt uneasy, all sixes and sevens. Maybe he should have gone with Antonio. At least he would have been with the big man if he didn't make it to the hospital.

Wracked by feelings of guilt for causing this latest disaster, angry at both himself and the Foreman, he cursed out loud. More than anything else he wanted revenge. That gave him pause. Was he any better than the Foreman? When it came right down to it, was he any different?

Fernando shook his head, trying to rid himself of these guilt feelings. He looked up at the ridge where the Foreman had fired down at them. Maybe, if he climbed the ridge, he could find out for sure if he'd wounded the Foreman and if so how badly. He checked his watch. It wouldn't take him more than a few minutes to scale the ridge. He would have plenty of time to catch up to Antonio at Christus Saint Vincent. Nothing happened fast in the Emergency Room. And it could take them hours to find an open operating room.

Fernando left his Steyr in the Cherokee and walked around behind the cabin. He followed a trail up through the ponderosa pines, enjoying the fragrance of the pine needles as he climbed the hill. He stopped when he saw the stand of aspen trees up ahead, just beyond the boulders. He waited, listening for any sound, as he was trained. Just in case the Foreman had an accomplice that he'd left behind to finish the dirty work he'd started. One down, one to go?

As he approached the aspens, he took out his Smith & Wesson. Like this he edged around the boulders to where he thought the Foreman had been standing. Sure enough, he found footprints among the trees, but only one set, not two. Searching the area he spotted a streak of blood on the pine needles. Behind him he saw telltale drops of blood leading into the forest.

So he had wounded the Foreman, but from what he'd seen so far it looked like a minor wound. Might not even need medical attention.

Fernando decided to follow the drops of blood for a short distance at least. So he holstered his Smith & Wesson and crept into the aspens. He continued to see drops of blood every few feet until he came to a fallen tree trunk. The ground around the tree was disturbed and part of a torn undershirt had been tossed on the ground. It looked like the Foreman had stopped to bandage his wound here. He looked but could not find any drops of blood beyond the tree trunk.

He debated what to do. If he tried to follow any further he would be late getting to the hospital to be with Antonio. It wasn't much of a decision. He needed to be with Antonio, for his sake as much as Antonio's.

So Fernando turned and headed down the hill.

16

Fernando walked into the Christus Saint Vincent Emergency Room a few minutes before six o'clock. Expecting the usual madhouse, he was surprised to find only a few people sitting in the waiting room, mostly older folks who tended to be quiet about what ailed them. No screaming kids or belligerent drunks this afternoon. Even the receptionist at the front counter seemed relaxed, all smiles while chatting to a colleague who stood behind her making copies at a photocopying machine.

"Can I help you?" she asked Fernando, a bouncy young woman with curly red hair and glasses.

"Yeah, I'm here for Sargent Antonio Blake," Fernando said. "He arrived by medevac about an hour ago. The medics asked me to provide whatever information I could."

"I think Detective Alvarez already gave us the information we need," she replied, looking at her computer screen.

"Okay, good," Fernando said. "Is he here now?"

The young woman nodded. "Yes, he's upstairs waiting in Mister Blake's room. That's three twenty. If he's not there, he's probably in the waiting room next to the ward. I believe Mister Blake is still in radiology."

"Thanks," Fernando said.

He took the elevator to the third floor. Manny wasn't in the waiting room outside the doors to the ward, so he walked onto the ward, passing the nurses station on his way to room 320.

Sure enough, he found Manny sitting in a chair next to the bed, cell phone in hand.

"What a coincidence," Manny said. "I was just about to call you. What the hell happened out there?"

Pulling up a chair, Fernando sat down next to Manny and began his explanation. "We set a trap for the Foreman at Antonio's cabin, but he outwitted us. He'd been following Antonio home from work, trying to find out where Antonio lived. So I had the bright idea that I would follow the two of them and pull in behind the Foreman when they reached the cabin. But the Foreman drove past Antonio's driveway. He found high ground above the cabin and ambushed us with his assault weapon. We returned fire, but Antonio got the worst of the exchange. I think I winged the Foreman, but he was still able to drive away."

"Jesus!" Manny said. "You're lucky you weren't hit. What about the Foreman? How do you know you wounded him?"

"I climbed up on the ridge where he was firing at us and found drops of blood," Fernando said. "Not a lot, but enough to cause him to run away. It's probably a minor wound."

Manny nodded. "Which means he'll be back."

While they talked, a nurse came into the room with the latest news. "Just wanted to let you know that Mister Blake is on his way to the operating room," she said, a heavy-set older woman with sad, heavy eyes. "Radiology found one bullet lacerated his liver and another nicked his large intestine."

Fernando shook his head. "What's the prognosis?"

The nurse sighed, as if tired of answering that question. "Depends on how much damage the bullet did to the liver. It's touch and go at this point. Mister Blake is in a lot of pain."

Neither Fernando nor Manny responded.

"The good news is that we found an open operating room," the nurse said. "We were able to reschedule an elective surgery. Anyway, you're both welcome to stay here during the surgery. Should take no more than two or three hours, and then you can visit him in the Intensive Care unit."

With that, the nurse turned and walked out of the room.

Fernando and Manny looked at each other.

"I guess I'll stay," Fernando said. "I caused this. It's my fault. The least I can do is stay with him until he's out of surgery and back in his room."

"Okay, I'll keep you company," Manny said.

So the waiting game began. They talked for a while and then took turns walking around the hospital. Later they went down to the cafeteria for a sandwich and a cold beverage. Fernando called Estelle from the cafeteria and explained what had happened and that he would be home late.

After they finished eating, they went back to Antonio's room and waited some more. Two hours passed and then three. Still no sign of a doctor.

As the end of the fourth hour approached, Fernando rose from his chair and walked to the door. "I'm going to look for one of the doctors.

Maybe they forgot all about us."

Manny laughed. "Good luck with that."

Fernando stepped outside the room and saw a doctor walking down the hall toward him. The doctor waved.

"I'm Doctor Yee, Mister Blake's surgeon," the doctor said, still wearing his green scrubs. "Everything went as well as could be expected. Now we'll just have to see how the liver heals. It's going to be a long recovery. He'll need help for a while after he's discharged."

"Will he survive?" Manny asked, bluntly.

The doctor hesitated. "Yes, we think his chances are good. Now if you'll excuse me, I have to return to the operating room. Mister Blake will be transferred to Intensive Care in just a few minutes."

They took the elevator down to the Intensive Care unit and waited outside the automatic doors for Antonio to arrive. A few minutes later the elevator opened and two orderlies wheeled out a gurney. At first Fernando didn't recognize Antonio. He looked somehow diminished on the gurney, pale and fragile and hooked to a network of monitors hanging on an IV pole. Antonio's eyes were closed, as though sound asleep. Or still unconscious.

Fernando and Manny waited in chairs outside the Intensive Care unit until they were given permission to enter. When they did, they found Antonio with his eyes still closed. The sight of Antonio so lifeless worried Fernando.

"His vitals are fine, he's just groggy from the surgery," one of the ICU nurses said, noticing Fernando's concern.

"Can he hear me?" Fernando asked.

The nurse nodded.

Fernando stepped up to the gurney and touched Antonio's arm. "Antonio...can you hear me? I'm sorry for what happened, old buddy."

Antonio's eyelids fluttered. He smiled faintly.

"I knew it–he's goldbricking!" Manny joked.

Antonio opened one eye and smiled again, this time more noticeably.

"You did good," Fernando said to Antonio. "You're gonna be fine."

Fernando and Manny stayed beside the gurney until the nurses kicked them off the unit, promising that Antonio would be in his room in about an hour.

"What do you think? Are you going to wait?" Manny asked.

Fernando checked his watch. "No, Estelle's waiting for me. I better get home. I'll be back tomorrow morning."

"Same here," Manny said. "I'll stop in tomorrow as soon as I can. Depends on what's popping down at the station."

They rode the elevator down to the ground floor and went their separate ways.

Fernando, still shaken, drove slowly and carefully to the Paseo and around to Acequia Madre. As he expected Estelle had been waiting up for him. She met him in the kitchen as soon as he walked through the door.

"How is he?" Estelle asked.

"Pretty bad," Fernando said.

Estelle have him a big hug. "It's not your fault, Fernando. You did the best you could."

Fernando said nothing, knowing it most certainly was his fault. The whole damn thing.

"I'm going to bed, it's late," Estelle said. "Do you want me to fix you something to eat before I go?"

Fernando shook his head. "No, I'm not hungry. I think I'll just go to bed. I'll be right there."

After Estelle went down the hall to their bedroom, Fernando walked into his study and sat at his desk in the darkness. Then he did something he hadn't done in many years. He wept.

17

Every morning that week Fernando drove down to Christus Saint Vincent to sit with Antonio, who grew stronger by the day. By midweek he was sitting up in bed and talking up a storm with the nurses. Toward the end of the week he was walking up and down the hallway asking for his discharge papers. On day five Fernando arrived late morning, when discharge orders were usually written, expecting to give Antonio a ride to his cabin in the Pecos.

When Fernando walked into Antonio's room that morning he was shocked to find two Antonios. Could he be seeing double? One Antonio sat in a chair beside the bed, the other stood at the foot of the bed, just as large and muscular as the first. Then he noticed that standing Antonio had a short-cropped beard on his lower jaw and wore a gray nylon exercise outfit that Sargent Antonio Blake wouldn't be caught dead wearing. Since leaving the military, Antonio was on record as saying he would never exercise again. Ever.

Both Antonios laughed at Fernando, who stood in the doorway bewildered.

"Fernando, this youngster is Daniel, my little brother," Antonio said from his chair.

"Little?" Fernando asked, the only thing he could think to say. Daniel looked as tall and as heavy as his big brother. Both of them could have been tight ends on a professional football team. The only difference was the short-cropped beard on Daniel's jaw.

"That's right, Daniel's the baby of the family," Antonio said. "He might not look it, but he's a good two inches shorter and twenty pounds lighter. I had to protect him when we were kids, he couldn't fight for shit."

"Okay, nice to meet you, Daniel," Fernando said, shaking hands with Daniel.

"Right back at you," Daniel said.

"I called him a couple of days ago and asked him to come down and help me get back on my feet," Antonio said, by way of explanation. "He lives in Denver, not far away."

"I get to babysit him for a change," Daniel said. "I tried to persuade him to come up to Denver for a few weeks while he recovered. I own a gym up there. He could work out and probably recover quicker."

"Yeah, but my doctors are all down here," Antonio said. "Plus I hate gyms. How many times do I have to tell you?"

Daniel turned to Fernando and rolled his eyes.

Fernando smiled at the two of them. He was happy for Antonio, who'd lived alone since a severe bout of PTSD had caused a nasty breakup of his marriage. Since his divorce Antonio always said he could never trust himself to live with another person, only alone.

"Good enough, then I'll turn him over to you," Fernando said to Daniel. "Do you guys need anything before I go?"

Daniel shook his head. "We should be fine...if he behaves himself."

Fernando laughed. "Good luck with that. Just give me a call if you need anything," Fernando said, handing Daniel one of his cards.

With that, Fernando left the hospital and drove to his office on Canyon Road. He felt relieved that Antonio would be looked after, but also a sense of disappointment. He'd enjoyed helping Antonio, as a kind of penance or atonement for indirectly causing his injury. A way to make amends to his oldest and best friend in the Santa Fe Police Department, a trusted colleague who had saved his ass more times than he cared to remember.

Also, worrying about Antonio had occupied his mind, providing a respite from brooding about the Foreman. With Daniel helping Antonio, Fernando's mind wandered back to the Foreman, who'd kept a low profile during the last week. He'd made no further attempts on anyone. The Foreman seemed to have disappeared, which both puzzled and worried Fernando.

So much so that Fernando began to wonder if he had seriously wounded the Foreman back at the cabin. Or was the Foreman just biding his time while planning another ambush? That seemed more likely. If so, where would he strike next?

These and other similar questions resurfaced as Fernando pulled into his parking lot. He stepped out of the Cherokee and looked around, half expecting to see the Foreman lurking in the shadows down by Essentia or in the empty lot on the other side of Canyon Road.

He hurried down the path to his office and opened the door. Once he got inside the familiar space he felt better. Safer, even though he knew very well that in his profession safety was an illusion.

Fernando put the 'Open' sign in his window and sat at his desk.

As always, he checked his messages. Only one message from a local real estate company wanting to sell him a house in a new subdivision near Tesuque. The last thing he needed. He took his laptop out of his top desk drawer and opened his spreadsheet folder. His numbers continued to go south. He hadn't had a paying customer in nearly a month. Fortunately, Ruby wasn't charging him rent. Good old Ruby. She was doing him an enormous favor, because rents on Canyon Road were out of this world, like the prices of houses in Santa Fe.

Come Noon Fernando decided to drive home for lunch. Maybe take the afternoon off and do some gardening, anything to get his mind off the Foreman. That plan lasted about two seconds.

As he exited his spreadsheet app his cell phone rang. He closed the laptop and then answered the phone.

"Mister Lopez, please help me!" came an unfamiliar and hysterical voice. "Can you please help me, I'm desperate. This is Joan Clark. He's following me. Right now. I'm scared to death. The Foreman, I mean. He's right behind me in his car, I don't know what to do. Please!"

Fernando recognized the voice now. "Okay, slow down. Tell me where you are, what's going on."

"He's following me," Joan said. "I went back to my house to pick up some clothes and he was waiting for me on the street. Remember, I told you he found out where I live. When I saw him sitting in his car I drove on by and headed for my friend's house on Hyde Park Road, where I've been staying. Then I came to my senses. I can't lead him to her house. That would be suicide, probably for the both of us. So I kept on driving up toward the ski basin. I'm almost there now. What'll I do? Please. Tell me what to do!"

Thinking quickly, Fernando said, "Okay, here's what I want you to do. Go all the way to the ski basin. Then turn around in the big parking lot and head back down the mountain as fast as you can. Don't let him get in front of you or cut you off. Don't worry about the speed limit. Just stay ahead of him."

"But where should I go?"

"Go back to your house," Fernando said. "Tell me where you live. I'll meet you there."

"I live in La Tierra," Joan said. "Just take Highway Two Eighty-five to Tano Road and then left on Loma Serena. I'm the third house on the left."

"That's almost to Tesuque, yes?"

"Not quite," Joan said.

"Is there a way I can get inside the house? An open door or window? A key you've hidden somewhere?"

"Yes, I keep a spare key under the rubber mat at the back entrance,"

Joan said. "It works on both the front and the back doors."

"Okay, I'll be inside the house waiting when you drive up," Fernando said. "I want you to park and run into the house as fast as you can. I'll open the door for you and take care of the Foreman."

"Thank you! Thank you! I'll pay whatever fee you charge."

"Don't worry about that now. Just get to your house safely."

Fernando didn't waste any time. He locked the office door and drove down to the Paseo and around to Highway 285. When he hit the highway he floored the Cherokee and raced down the highway to Tano Road, where the intersection forced him to slow down. Once on Tano Road it took him several minutes to find Loma Serena. When he did, he drove past the third house on the left and parked around a curve, where the Cherokee couldn't be seen from Loma Serena. Then he took off running as fast as he could toward Joan's house.

This time he would be the one doing the ambushing.

18

Fernando ran down the long driveway toward Joan's house. He half expected Joan and the Foreman's cars to arrive before he could get inside the house, a new frame building constructed from particle board and chicken wire and covered with brown stucco to look like an authentic adobe. Whereas Adobe houses could last hundreds of years, this newbie would be lucky to last ten years before it came apart at the seams. That was his impression as he hurried through a rock and cactus garden along the left side of the house, taking care to step on the widely scattered flagstones that zig-zagged through the garden.

He found a small brick patio behind the house, complete with a cast iron table and chairs with a bright blue umbrella overhanging the furniture. Immediately he saw what made the location attractive to people willing to spend the money to buy a new house in Santa Fe. The view of the Tesuque hills framed by the Sangre de Cristo Mountains took his breath away. Not bad, if you were willing to live in a particle board and chicken wire house.

Fernando went directly to the porch. Under a black rubber mat he found the house key Joan had promised. With key in hand, he unlocked the door, a fancy wooden door painted brown with a partial stained glass window in its top half. Then he stepped into a kitchen with white walls and all new, white appliances. Not stopping to gawk, he walked down a short hallway, past two bedrooms, into a large living/dining area. The living area offered a bit more color, with a Georgia O'Keeffe poster and a couple of original paintings of Native American dancers and pueblos hanging on the white walls. Everywhere white. Maybe Joan liked white because she was a nurse. Then he remembered that nurses didn't normally wear white these days.

He hurried to the front door, hoping to have a few minutes to come up with a strategy. He still hadn't decided how to play this. His recent experience at Antonio's cabin didn't give him much confidence in his ability to make a plan now that would actually work, but he needed something, a place to start. First thing, he wanted to get Joan inside the house as quickly as possible. Once she was safe, then he could worry about confronting the Foreman when he arrived. Get her to safety first, that was all he could come up with.

Just then Fernando heard a car barreling down Loma Serena Street. He brushed aside the curtains on the front door window and watched Joan's red Sentra come barreling down the street and swerving into the driveway. He stepped back from the door, thinking she was going to crash into the house. Instead, the Sentra skidded to a stop a few feet from the porch. Before getting out of the Sentra, Joan opened the glove compartment and grabbed something. As soon as she opened the car door to get out, all hell broke loose.

The white ghost came swerving into the driveway and screeched to a stop behind the Sentra. The Foreman jumped out of the white ghost waving what looked like a Glock pistol. "Stop or I'll shoot!" he barked, wearing his usual khaki uniform.

As Fernando watched from the front door window, frozen in place, Joan turned to face the brutish Foreman. "Leave me alone!" she screamed.

"You ratted me out, you fucking bitch!" he shouted back at her.

"You got what you deserved," she said, wearing a gray sweater and black tights, with an Isotopes baseball cap pulled down over her forehead.

"Hah!" the Foreman shot back. "What about you? Did you get what you deserved? You're the one who drugged the girls and primped them for sex. You sent them in to be abused, you and no one else."

Joan's shoulders slumped. She staggered, as if she'd been slapped across the face. "I did what I could. I tried to help."

"Help? How's that? By sending them in to be sodomized?"

Joan burst into tears. She turned to run into the house but the Foreman was too fast for her. He bounded over and grabbed her from behind. Then he threw his thick left arm around her neck, choking her.

Fernando noticed a small bandage on the Foreman's left forearm, just above the wrist. The bullet he fired back at Antonio's cabin?

Now the scene before him shifted into slow motion.

Joan screamed.

The Foreman waved the pistol in her face, threatening to hit her.

Then Joan lowered her right arm, holding something in her hand. With one quick movement she turned to her right and shoved her right hand back into the Foreman's groin.

The Foreman cursed and let go of her, pushing her away. He grabbed his groin and bent over cursing.

Fernando seized the moment. He jumped out of the door, grabbed

Joan by the arm, and pulled her inside the house.

Seeing Fernando rescuing Joan, the Forman lunged upright and started shooting: Pop! Pop! Pop!

The bullets shattered the window on the front door and splintered the door. Pieces of glass and wood showered Fernando and Joan, who huddled together on the floor of the hallway.

As soon as the Foreman stopped firing, Fernando sprang to his feet. He threw open the door and fired his Smith & Wesson at the Foreman, who had already climbed into the white ghost and started the engine: Pop! Pop! Pop! The front windshield of the Audi burst into a thousand pieces of glass.

Ducking in the driver's seat, the Foreman spun the white car around and shot up the driveway, bouncing over the curb and spinning out of control. The Audi smashed into a mailbox across the street before the Foreman could get control and steer it back onto the street. Then the Foreman sped off toward Tano Road.

Fernando followed the Foreman into the driveway, firing repeatedly: Pop! Pop! Pop! His bullets pinged off the rear of the white ghost as it crested a small rise and turned onto Tano Road. At that point Fernando stopped shooting for fear of hitting a nearby house or a passing car. He ran up the driveway and watched the white ghost disappear in traffic on Tano Road, all he could do. Then he went back to the house to check on Joan.

She stood in the center of the living room now, mute. In her hand she held a bloody surgical scalpel. That was what she took out of her glove compartment, Fernando realized. And that was what she jabbed into the Foreman's groin. Good for her.

"Are you okay?" he asked.

Joan nodded. "I'm just angry now. I want him to be gone. I want him to be dead and gone."

"You're not alone," Fernando said. "But in the meantime, here's what I want you to do. Get your biggest suitcase, pack enough clothes to last you a week, and then go back to your friend's house. And stay put. Don't come back here until we have him in custody. It's just a matter of time. I'll call you when we have him in custody."

"What if he follows me now?" she asked. "He could be waiting for me up the street?"

Fernando shook his head. "He won't, because I'll be right behind you. Trust me. I'll follow you all the way to Hyde Park Road. If he follows you, I'll shoot the bastard, okay?"

She nodded tentatively. "What about the door," she said, pointing to the broken window and the bullet holes in the door.

"Not a problem. I'll send my door and window man over to fix it," Fernando said, almost laughing, because old Dick was getting a lot of business thanks to the trigger-happy Foreman. "His name is Dick Murphy. He owns Dick's Door and Window. He'll fix the broken window and repair or replace the door. I'll tell him about the key under the back door mat. It'll be as good as new when you return."

"Okay," she said, nodding. "I'll get my clothes."

Fernando waited at the front door while Joan packed a suitcase. When she returned, he carried her suitcase out to the Sentra. Then he followed her around to the entrance to Hyde Park Road. He pulled off on the shoulder and waited at the entrance. He watched her disappear up the winding road toward the ski basin, his Smith & Wesson on the passenger's seat, ready and waiting. He wished the Foreman would appear so he could get this over with, one way or the other. He was damn tired of waiting around day after day. When the Foreman hadn't appeared after an hour, he called it quits and drove off, heading back to his office.

By now the Foreman had been both shot in the arm and stabbed in the groin, which was enough to discourage most people. But knowing the Foreman, Fernando doubted he would ever stop his personal revenge tragedy until he and/or his jailors were dead.

The only question now was where and who the Foreman would strike next.

19

Back in his office Fernando called Dick Murphy and asked if he could do an emergency repair job on Joan's front door. Murphy agreed to do it that afternoon and evening, if Fernando would pay his emergency fee, fifty percent more than his regular fee. Since Joan would pay for the repair, Fernando said sure, whatever you need. Dick said he probably could have a door installed by nightfall, but it would only be a holder, a generic wooden or metal door until she could go to Home Depot and order whatever she wanted.

"All the decent front doors are only available by order," Dick said. "And expensive as all get out."

"Good enough," Fernando said. "You'll find a key under the rubber mat on the back porch. It opens both the front and back doors."

"I'll do my best to install the door, but if it's wood I won't be able to paint it tonight," Dick said.

"Okay, that's fine, if you can get a new door installed today the owner will be happy," Fernando said. You can paint the door later, whatever it needs. As long as the door is secure, that's all that counts."

"Will do," Dick said and clicked off.

Fernando checked the time. He smiled when he saw that Happy Hour had already begun at El Farol. Just what he needed after another long, stressful day.

So he locked up his office and walked down Canyon Road to El Farol. An old geezer he didn't recognize sat at one of the tables on the porch as he made his way up the steps and into the trendy restaurant. Paul, the head bartender, nodded as he walked up to the bar looking for friendly faces. Paul pointed toward the restaurant part of El Farol, through the arched doorway.

Ruby waved at him from a table next to the brightly colored mural of Flamenco dancers on the wall. Sunlight coming in the window behind her splashed Ruby with the red, green, and yellow shades of the mural. As usual, she sat at the table with two of the other regulars, Blaine Rogers and Dave Stein. Blaine gave him the finger and Dave mumbled something out of the side of his mouth, something sarcastic no doubt. Fernando took no offence. He'd long ago gotten used to the sarcastic sense of humor and ribald ways of the artistic crowd.

Ruby checked her wristwatch. "You're late."

"Been a long day," Fernando said, sitting next to Ruby and across the table from Blaine.

"Yeah? What's happened now?" Ruby asked.

"Oh for the love of God, spare us the details about your depressing detective work," Blaine said. Today the big man wore a Grateful Dead T-shirt under his fishing vest and over his red Bermuda shorts, the only gallery owner in town who dressed like...like what? Fernando couldn't even describe the Blaine Rogers look. His Picasso and Co. gallery was just as bizarre.

"What'd he say?" Dave said, a 90-year-old artist who at one time painted. Now nobody knew what he did when he wasn't at El Farol. He spoke in short bursts out of the corner of his mouth. When he did, he always sounded like a toad croaking: 'Ribbit. Ribbit.'

"Shut the fuck up, Blaine. This is happy hour, so be happy!" Ruby lectured Blaine. The two of them were well matched.

Blaine bolted up from the table–all six feet, four inches and two hundred fifty pounds of him–and yelled at the server to bring another round of margaritas for him and Ruby. The only person in Santa Fe more intimidating than Blaine was Antonio. The two big men were arch enemies.

Meanwhile, Dave had both hands wrapped around a long-neck Budweiser. He usually nursed one beer all afternoon.

Eventually Patty, one of the afternoon servers, brought the two margaritas and a Modelo draft for Fernando. All the servers at El Farol knew that Fernando drank only Modelo.

Ruby kept looking at the doorway. "I'm waiting for Athena Doering, I don't know if she's going to show up or not. She's having trouble with her fucking husband. He beat her up again last night."

"Sonny Davis?" Fernando asked.

"That's him," Ruby said. "He's a real bastard. Likes to beat up women."

Blaine laughed. "Hah! He's a pussy! I'd like to teach him a thing or two about his manners with women."

Fernando shook his head. "I've seen them here, but I don't really know either of them."

Ruby made a face of disgust. "They bought the old Moon Gallery about six years ago. They're quite a pair. Filthy rich. That is, Athena's filthy rich. Her first husband was a vice president at Procter and Gamble in Cincinnati. He died of a heart attack a few years ago and left Athena millions of dollars in stock and real estate. After her husband died, Athena dropped out of stuffy Cincinnati high society and took a young lover and then made the mistake of marrying him. That would be Sonny."

Fernando frowned. "What do you know about Sonny...other than he's a wife beater?"

Ruby laughed. "He's the exact opposite of Athena, a low-class English soccer hooligan who married Athena for her money. He's younger than she is, a womanizer and heavy drinker, a real piece of shit. He was one of the Johns who frequented Three Hills Ranch, where Robert Warner provided him with underage girls to fuck. People around here think it was just outsiders who abused those young girls, but plenty of the predators were rich guys from Santa Fe who live in gated communities around town. The gentrification swine. You remember that crowd, right?"

Fernando nodded. "I know, but I can't remember seeing Sonny's name in the court papers after we busted Three Hills Ranch," Fernando said. "So what did Athena find attractive about this guy?"

"His youth," Ruby said. "Sex with a young lover. I suppose that excited Athena until Sonny started getting rough with her. Now she's trying to divorce the bastard, but he wants half of her money."

"Let me have a few minutes with him in a closed room, I'll send him packing," Blaine said, full of alcohol-fueled bravado.

"I don't know, Blaine," Ruby said doubtfully. "You're getting a little long in the tooth to take on a younger soccer player, even if Sonny is an out-of-shape drunk. Come to think of it, you are too."

"Hah!" Blaine bellowed. "Are you questioning my physical prowess? You should know better than that."

"Hah yourself!" Ruby shot back. "Just because you're good in bed doesn't mean you're Mohammad Ali."

While Ruby and Blaine bickered, the door to El Farol opened and in walked Athena Doering.

"She made it. All right," Ruby said, walking over to meet Athena, a heavy-set woman with shoulder-length gray hair wearing an expensive tailored suit of what looked like maroon suede. Her heavy make-up failed to cover the bruises on her cheeks and neck. Her sunglasses only partly hid a swollen left eye, bruised black and blue. She limped, favoring her right leg.

"Jesus, Athena, you need to get a restraining order on that sonofabitch husband of yours!" Ruby said.

"I did finally, just this afternoon," Athena said. "He took all his stuff and moved out, but he's threatening to kill me unless I give him half of my estate, including our gallery. He wants the gallery so he can keep working there."

Ruby turned to Fernando. "Can't you do something to help?"

Fernando introduced himself to Athena. "We haven't met formally, but I'm a private investigator, former police detective here in Santa Fe. Maybe I could help, I don't know."

Athena looked at Fernando, sizing him up. "Maybe you could. Do you have a card?"

"Yes," Fernando said, handing her one of his cards.

She read the card and looked at Fernando again. "So what kinds of things do you do?"

"Whatever's required," Fernando said.

Athena smiled. With her eyes hidden behind dark sunglasses and her swollen face masked by black and blue bruises, her curled lips looked almost grotesque.

20

Next morning Fernando got up early and made a big breakfast for Estelle to celebrate her homecoming: a vegie omelet with homemade link sausages from their local butcher. He microwaved a couple of frozen croissants and had everything ready and on the table when she came into the kitchen, already dressed for work. Estelle paused a moment. She cast a suspicious glance at the new front windows. She walked over to the windows and ran her finger across the glass looking for dust but said nothing. Fortunately she didn't notice the newly painted patches on the walls and cabinets. Don't ask, don't tell seemed to work just fine as they got older. And if he added a home-cooked country breakfast, Fernando figured he would be off the hook.

Over breakfast Fernando gave her an update on Antonio's condition, as far as he knew.

Estelle nodded and asked, "Is he going to be all right?"

"I think so," Fernando said. "But he'll have a long recovery. At least that's what I've been told."

"What about you?" Estelle asked. "Are you going to keep chasing this guy and putting yourself in harm's way?"

Fernando shrugged. "Only if he comes after me."

Estelle glanced at him, not pleased with his evasive answer.

In truth, he hadn't told Estelle about most of his encounters with the Foreman. On purpose. He knew very well what her reaction would be. He didn't want to repeat that conversation.

Estelle left for work right after breakfast, leaving him to clean up the kitchen and make the bed. He didn't mind his newfound domesticity. It kept his mind from going to the dark side: worrying about Antonio's condition, the Foreman's whereabouts, and a list of other troubles.

After he showered and dressed in clean clothes, he locked up and left the house. He fired up the Cherokee and drove around the Paseo to his office on Canyon Road. As he pulled into the parking lot he saw Ruby talking to the Bryans over in front of Essentia, their sex shop. They waved.

Fernando waved back.

He walked down the gravel path to his office and opened the door. He noticed the light on his answering machine right away. After he placed the 'Open' sign in his front window, he sat at his desk and hit the playback button:

"Mister Lopez...this is Athena Doering. After giving it some thought, I think you may be able to help me. Would you please call me back at this number? The sooner the better."

The voice was cold, calculating. She didn't sound like a damsel in distress. Still, he dialed her number to see what she wanted.

Athena answered right away. "Thanks for calling back," she said, in a friendlier tone of voice.

"No problem," Fernando said. "I'm willing to do what I can. I'll send you my rate card."

"Don't worry about that," Athena said. "I'll pay you whatever you want."

"So what can I do for you?" he asked.

"I want Sonny gone. I want him to disappear," she said.

Fernando paused. He wanted to choose his words carefully in case Athena was recording the conversation. Very carefully. "Okay...I understand...you want Sonny out of your life...so what exactly do you want him to do?"

"Well," Athena started and then stopped. She sighed. "If you put it that way, I want him to accept the settlement my lawyer proposed and sign the divorce papers. I offered him half a million dollars and possession of the gallery. He loves that gallery, he's king of the roost there with all the young women he hires. Let him have it. I'm returning to Cincinnati as soon as the papers are signed. I have family and friends there. I just want to be rid of him, you understand?"

"Of course," Fernando said.

"You do this for me–get rid of him–and you can name your price," she said. "Money is no problem."

Fernando smiled, not used to hearing that. "Okay. You said earlier that Sonny had moved out. Where is he staying now?"

"He's staying at La Fonda, but you can find him at the gallery during the day, Monday through Saturday," Athena said. "Sometimes he even sleeps there. He has a Taos sofa in his office, probably so he can have relations with the young bimbos he likes to surround himself with. I don't know, and I don't care, as long as he disappears from my life."

"That's all I need. I'll be in touch," Fernando said and hung up the phone before the conversation could take a legally dangerous turn.

He sat at his desk for a good long while. The more he thought about it, the more he liked his assignment. It would certainly be lucrative, which is what he needed to balance his books. He'd been running on credit for months, taking one *pro bono* case after another. Like everyone else, he needed to be paid. And Athena Doering would pay him well.

It was clear from their conversation that Athena wanted Sonny dead, or at least preferred to have Sonny dead. That made no difference to Fernando. Lots of estranged spouses probably felt the same way. But he was no paid assassin, which meant he would have to find another way to get rid of Sonny. It shouldn't be that difficult. Half a million dollars and an expensive gallery on Canyon Road wasn't anything to scoff at. Hard to believe Sonny would turn that down and risk coming away empty handed at the end of an expensive, nasty divorce trial in which a low-life like Sonny would have no chance whatsoever against a wealthy socialite like Athena Doering and all her lawyers.

Fernando first had to decide where to confront Sonny. At his room in La Fonda? Or at his gallery? His room would be more private, but there he would run the risk of tangling with La Fonda security. What's more, something about the gallery appealed to Fernando. Maybe it would be better to confront him in public, where Sonny would have to control his anger so as to not make a fool of himself. Embarrass him in front of his bimbos, maybe even his customers, so much that he would agree to accept the settlement just to end the embarrassment. That just might work.

Now or later? He decided there was no time like the present. He needed the money now.

So after buckling on his Smith & Wesson, Fernando locked the office and walked down Canyon Road to Athena Gallery, which sat back from Canyon Road about fifty feet. The sculpture garden in front drew you to the front door, through a walkway of Greek and Roman themed marble statues mixed with a few Native American bronzes. The surrounding plantings and flower gardens were so immaculately tended they looked English. The gallery screamed money, even before you entered the building with its pale beige stucco that seemed to radiate light and its front door painted bright blue to ward off evil spirits, according to local lore.

Fernando opened the door and stepped inside a glowing palace of color. Huge oil paintings hung from the walls in meticulous arrangement, with each painting given enough space to make it stand out individually. Huge paintings, as large as area rugs: five by seven, six by eight, and two enormous red paintings that took up the entire rear wall. All modernist abstracts that could have been on loan from a major gallery. Walking through the front room Fernando didn't see a single painting for sale under five digits. It was clear to him that Athena Gallery catered to a very small crowd: the filthy rich, whether they be tourists or local Santa Feans.

Not surprisingly, the two women clerks behind the counter looked like professional models: young, blond, thin, and dressed as if they were on their way to the Oscars' Red Carpet, even if they were more likely to end up on Sonny's bed than any red carpet. Fernando saw a third blonde inside a small office, sitting on a desk facing a middle-aged man in the chair behind the desk. The man, who Fernando recognized as Sonny Davis, had his hand on the woman's thigh under her skirt. The young woman smiled back at Sonny, apparently not minding the carnal attention. Or pretending not to mind.

A full-service bar took up most of the rear wall, complete with bottles of wine and hard liquor. An open bottle of champagne and two long-stem glasses remained on the desk from whatever foreplay was going on before Fernando entered. A Taos bed with rumpled blankets took up most of a side wall. It wasn't hard to guess the purpose of the Taos bed.

Frowning, Fernando barged into the office without announcing himself. "So sorry to interrupt your party, Sonny."

"Aye, mate, what can we do for you?" Sonny asked, seemingly unaffected by Fernando's rudeness. Instead, Sonny smiled broadly, a once handsome man who had clearly gone to seed, with a pot belly and the puffy, flaccid face of a serious alcoholic. With close-cropped hair and gray stubble on his face, he wore a red jersey with three white pinstripes on the shoulders and a red and blue FC Cincinnati logo in front. Tight black jeans and a silver chain around his neck completed his laid-back, retired athlete look.

Fernando smiled when he saw Sonny's physical condition. Not much to fear from a pudgy drunk.

The young woman's face turned bright red. She pulled Sonny's hand out from under her skirt and excused herself. She hurried out of the office, smoothing her skirt as she fled.

Fernando handed Sonny his card. "Fernando Lopez. I'm a private investigator, some call me a fixer."

Sonny chuckled. "Yeah? What's a fixer do?"

"I fix whatever I'm paid to fix," Fernando said.

Now Sonny looked concerned. "I suppose you're workin' for my feckin' wife then."

Fernando nodded. "She's finished with you, Sonny. The marriage is over. She wants you to sign the settlement that's on the table and be gone from her life forever. You comprend?"

Sonny's mood changed instantly. He turned sullen, hostile. "*Ni*," he said.

"I assume that's Celtic for 'no.' You are Irish, right?"

"Yeah, but I moved to England when I was young," Sonny said. "Better football. I played for Portsmouth for a good ten years until I busted up me knee."

Fernando pointed to Sonny's jersey. "How'd you get to Cincinnati?"

"Coach lined me up with a position on the Cinci team," Sonny said. "I could coach some and play with me bum knee there because the competition ain't that good over here, you know."

"So I'm told," Fernando said. "And you met your wife in Cincinnati."

Sonny frowned. "Fancy that."

"Quite a success story," Fernando said. "A broken down athlete marries old money."

"*Innit*, though," Sonny shot back.

"So much money that you were able to enjoy all the young girls Robert Warner kept locked up at Three Hills Ranch," Fernando continued. "Young girls you paid for and sexually abused, just like you abuse your wife."

Sonny stared at Fernando with fire in his eyes. "I was never charged...."

Fernando cut him off. "Of course not, you have too much money. Or rather, your wife has too much money. You have nothing, *nada*. You're a has-been jock with no prospects."

Angry now, Sonny shot back, "What do you want?"

"Well, here's the thing, Sonny boy," Fernando said. "You're going to sign the papers and accept your wife's offer of half a million dollars and this gallery you love so much. You can keep fucking all the young women you hire to be your playmates here, as long as they're not underage. You'd have to be crazy to turn down the offer, a broken-down drunk like you. If you play your cards right, you won't have to work another day in your life–if you've ever worked a day in your life, which I seriously doubt, looking at you now."

"Listen–" Sonny said, trying to rise up out of his desk chair.

Fernando pushed Sonny back in the chair with his left hand while pulling out his Smith & Wesson with his right. He shoved the barrel of the pistol hard against Sonny's forehead. "You're gonna sign the papers and take your half million! And if you ever lay your hands on your wife or any other woman again, it'll be the last time you ever touch anyone!"

With that, Fernando kicked the chair and sent it and Sonny crashing into the table along the back wall, sending glasses and bottles crashing down. The floor exploded with broken glass and booze. Then Fernando turned and walked out of the gallery, while Sonny's three blond bimbos watched him.

All three of them were smiling.

21

Fernando had absolutely no doubt in his mind that Sonny boy would follow orders. Like all men who beat women, Sonny was a fucking coward. He had no appetite for the rough stuff. Plus, Sonny had to know that no judge or jury in this country would side with a drunken, wife-beating interloper over a woman like Athena Doering. The cards were stacked against him. Even a drunken has-been soccer player was smart enough to know that.

Sure enough, Athena called later that afternoon to tell Fernando that Sonny had signed the papers. "I'm sending you a check," she said.

"Do you want me to send you an invoice?" Fernando asked, calculating what he could reasonably charge her.

"How's twenty thousand sound to you?" Athena asked.

Taken aback by her generosity, Fernando remained silent.

"Okay, then, how about twenty-five?" she asked.

"Thanks, that would be very generous," Fernando said. He wasn't about to complain.

"No. Thank you. You've given me a new life," she said, hanging up.

Fernando knew he hadn't earned anything close to twenty-five thousand dollars for his five-minute conversation–if you want to call it that–with Sonny boy. Still, he felt a sense of relief that he would finally be able to balance his spreadsheets. Too many *pro bono* clients over the last couple of months had put him deeply in the red. Now he would be able to pay off his credit cards and cover his travel expenses. Estelle would be happy, as would Ruby. He hadn't been able to pay his share of their utility bills these past few months.

Later that afternoon he decided to pay Antonio a visit. He wanted to check on the big man's recovery, now that he was home in his rustic cabin, which wasn't exactly the ideal place to recover from a serious wound. So he locked his office and drove the Cherokee around the Paseo to Old Santa Fe Trail. He found himself glancing repeatedly in the rear view mirror, checking to see if the white ghost was behind him. Call him paranoid, but he wanted to be prepared if and when the Foreman reappeared. He feared he would have this compulsion until the Foreman was history. Captured or killed, one way or the other.

He glanced in the rear view mirror one last time as he steered onto the road to Antonio's cabin. Turning into the drive he saw Antonio's Jeep parked up close to the door of the cabin. He pulled up under a huge ponderosa pine off to the side of the cabin so as not to block the Jeep. As he killed the Cherokee's big engine and set the brake, Antonio's brother Daniel stepped out of the cabin and walked down the drive to meet Fernando.

Daniel waved. "Good to see you. I'm having a helluva time convincing Antonio to take it easy. He wants to go back to work already."

Fernando laughed. "Sounds like Antonio."

"I mean, they told him to take a month off, whatever he needed," Daniel said. "He's so damned stubborn."

Antonio heard them talking and came slowly out of the cabin to join them. Fernando noticed right away that Antonio had lost more weight. He looked better than he did back at the hospital, but still somewhat feeble. He had a cane in his right hand that he leaned on when walking.

"You've lost weight, Antonio," Fernando said.

"That's because he doesn't know how to cook," Antonio replied, waving the cane at his brother.

"Hah! He eats like a horse, I can't fill him up."

Antonio shook his head. "I need to start going to the Shed with Fernando for my usual lunch."

"Maybe we can stop there after your doctor's appointment tomorrow morning," Daniel said.

"Yeah, because I need something edible for a change," Antonio said.

Daniel waved him off.

"What does the doctor say?" Fernando asked.

Antonio shrugged. "Not much, you know how doctors are. He seems to think I'll get back to where I was. It'll just take time."

"Hell, I could have told you that," Fernando said.

Antonio laughed. "And charged me less than he did, I'm sure."

"Come on into the cabin for a beer," Daniel said.

Fernando and Antonio followed Daniel into the cabin. Antonio sat in his leather recliner, his only extravagance in his otherwise Spartan lifestyle.

Fernando took a seat on one of the handmade wooden chairs. Fortunately the chair came with a seat cushion, which made sitting on it tolerable. The cabin was exactly the way Antonio wanted it: primitive. A couple of small tables and a bookcase completed his living area. The so-called kitchen had a wood burning stove and a heavy-duty REI cooler on the counter. With no electricity, Antonio depended on battery-operated Coleman lanterns. He had a solar panel on the roof to charge his cell phone and recharge his batteries. The bathroom consisted of a wooden outhouse out back behind the cabin. To Fernando, Antonio's shack was only one small step up from bear claw man's cabin.

Daniel reached down in the cooler and brought up three beers. He passed them out and sat down on the second wooden chair. "I hope you don't have any standards, because he drinks this Santa Fe Pale Ale shit," Daniel said. "Plus, it's not exactly cold, given the quality of his refrigeration."

"Only as a substitute for Modelo," Fernando said.

"Fuck off, both of you," Antonio said.

Fernando looked around the cabin. He saw Daniel's cache of weapons on a long table across the room: a pistol, boxes of ammo, and what looked like a bullet-proof vest. Standing upright against the table was none other than a Barrett MRAD sniper's rifle. Fernando hadn't seen one of those in years. A six thousand dollar weapon intended for professionals who did some serious shooting. Daniel must know his way around weapons. That made Fernando feel better about Antonio and Daniel being all alone here with the Foreman on the loose.

"Have you had any trouble...or seen any sign of the Foreman?" Fernando asked.

Antonio shook his head. "Not around here."

"Yeah, but I saw him in Pecos yesterday," Daniel interrupted. "I'm sure it was him. I had to go into town for groceries. On the way back I saw the white Audi coming down Highway Sixty-three into Pecos. He turned right on Highway Fifty, so I followed him all the way back here. I thought he was going to stop, but he didn't. Instead he continued driving toward Santa Fe."

Fernando frowned, troubled by the news. "What was he doing in Pecos?"

Daniel shrugged. "Don't know. He was coming down Highway Sixty-three from the north, that's all I know."

"What's up there, grocery stores where he could have gone shopping for supplies?" Fernando asked.

"No, the grocery stores are all in the center of town," Daniel said. "Maybe a convenience store, I don't know."

Fernando remembered the bear claw man telling him and Jodie the Foreman was staying somewhere in the woods. As he said that, the bear claw man motioned east toward Pecos and Highway Sixty-three.

"What's up Highway Sixty-three north of Pecos?" Daniel asked.

"Nothing, just national forest," Antonio said.

"That's the road to Cowles," Fernando added. "Lots of campgrounds and recreational sites up there."

Antonio shook his head. "Like I said. Nothing."

22

Fernando spent the morning paying his overdue bills, after Athena transferred $25,000 to his business banking account. First, though, he presented Estelle with a $2,000 check for the Saint Francis Immigrant Outreach Program she worked for, thinking the donation would garner some good will and let him off the hook as he finished this business with the Foreman. Not to put too fine a point on it: a bribe! He needed all the good will he could get. Dealing with the Foreman had been messy and was bound to get worse.

When he handed Estelle the check, she came over and kissed him on the cheek and then said, "That's fine, but I still want you to close your business and really retire. You're too old to be chasing killers around the countryside."

Too old? Fernando brooded on that as Estelle walked out of the kitchen and drove off to work. Maybe so, but he had to put an end to this nightmare he'd been living. It started years ago at Three Hills Ranch and still haunted him: all those young women held captive, prisoners to be offered up as sex slaves to depraved men like Sonny Davis. Robert Warner and the Foreman abused and even killed them if they tried to escape. The faces of the young women haunted him to this day, reminding him of his own daughters and how he would feel if Flavia and Adela were among the captives. He needed closure so that he could move on. He wasn't a quitter, never had been. No, he intended to see this through to the bitter end, whatever that would bring. Estelle would just have to understand.

Later he drove down to his office and parked beside Ruby's Accord. He bypassed his office and walked into Ruby's gallery. He found her standing at the front counter pricing pieces of pottery, colorful bowls and pitchers and platters made by friends at the pottery co-op she ran in the Railyard District.

Ruby threw down her pen when she saw Fernando. "Oh, hell, I don't know what I'm doing," she said to Fernando. "All these prices are arbitrary. What's a platter worth these days?"

Fernando smiled. "You could sell them by the pound...kind of like a grocery store."

Ruby gave him a dirty look. "So how've you been? I haven't had time to talk to you much lately," she said, looking like she'd just come from her potter's wheel at the co-op, wearing jeans and a black T-shirt smudged with gray clay. Her long, luxurious black hair was tucked under a baseball cap.

"Yeah, busy with this Foreman business," Fernando said. "Three Hills Ranch just won't go away."

"Nasty stuff," Ruby agreed. "All those old fucks who went there to rape those girls should be in jail. Every last one of them."

"Wouldn't it be nice," Fernando said. "Hey, I've got some good news. I can pay my utility bills."

"Hot damn! What, did your horse come in at the Santa Fe Downs?" Ruby asked, winking at him.

Fernando laughed. "No, one of my clients finally paid me."

"About time! You have to stop the *pro bono* crap," Ruby said.

'I know," Fernando said. "Problem is, most of the people who come to see me have less money than I do."

Ruby nodded. "Same with the co-op. I used to charge my ladies for space, but now I just let them use the studio free of charge. What the hell? They help me out, I help them out. We're all in this together, right?"

"Most of us, anyway," Fernando said. "So how about you put the price tags away for now and we go to lunch at El Farol? My treat. It's the least I can do considering I haven't paid my utilities for several months now."

Ruby laughed. "I guess I better take you up on that. I might not ever get another offer from you."

He waited at the counter while Ruby went into the restroom in back to wash the clay smudges off her face and T-shirt. When she returned, she had wet patches instead of clay smudges on her T-shirt. "I guess this looks okay," Ruby said, looking at her wet T-shirt.

"At our age everyone ignores us anyway," Fernando said. "We're like the potted plant in back of El Farol. Just there."

Ruby laughed.

They walked down the street to El Farol and ordered lunch. Fernando gave Ruby an update on Antonio and then told her about the work he'd done for Athena. He told her that Sonny had agreed to Athena's terms and signed the divorce papers. She had to give Sonny the gallery and half a million dollars, but she got rid of him and kept most of her money.

"How did you get him to do that?" Ruby asked.

Fernando chuckled. "I made him an offer he couldn't refuse."

Ruby gave him a look. "One of your famous offers, eh?"

After Fernando paid the bill, they walked back up Canyon Road. As they approached their parking lot Fernando noticed a Santa Fe County Sheriff's cruiser parked next to his Cherokee. "Now what?" he asked.

"Not again, don't tell me," Ruby said. "Someone broke into my gallery the day before yesterday looking for cash. They rifled through my desk and busted my cash register. I had to order a new one this morning."

"What did they take?" Fernando asked.

Ruby laughed. "Two pots. I don't keep any cash in the gallery, so they grabbed a couple of pots on their way out. Can you believe that? Two pots. What a bunch of dumb asses."

Fernando walked up to the empty cruiser and looked inside. He saw no one in the cruiser. He didn't see anyone in the parking lot either, so Ruby walked up on the porch of her gallery and opened her door. Fernando waited while she stepped inside the gallery and looked around. She reappeared a few moments later.

"The gallery's clear," Ruby reported. "Check your office. And be careful, Fernando."

Fernando did as she advised. He took out his Smith & Wesson and eased on down the path to his office. He approached the door carefully, trying not to make any noise, which was difficult walking on gravel. He peered through the side window and was surprised to see Jodie sitting in the chair across from his desk. Did he forget to lock the door? He couldn't remember. Sure enough, when he tried the door he found it unlocked.

Fernando stepped inside the office. "Jodie. How'd you get in?"

Jodie dangled a lock pick from her right hand. She wore civvies today, jeans and a black sports jersey that showed her muscles and her curves. "I took the liberty. We have an emergency on our hands. I need your help."

"Okay...shoot."

"Oh I plan to," she said, with a serious look on her face. "Sharon and I were supposed to meet for lunch at Pronzo this morning at eleven thirty. You know, the Italian restaurant off Johnson Street. Moved there from the Railyard District a few years back."

Fernando nodded. "She wasn't teaching today?"

"Not on Saturday," Jodie said.

Fernando realized he'd lost track of the day. After retiring, it was hard to distinguish one day from another.

"I waited for over an hour, but Sharon never showed," Jodie continued. "Nor did she answer her phone. I expected the worse, so I rushed back to our house on Nine Mile Road. I found our front door smashed open and the hallway a mess of broken glass and furniture. On the kitchen table I found Sharon's cell phone and this."

Jodie held out her hand.

Fernando hurried to his desk and sat down. Jodie handed him a sheet of white paper. Scrawled across the paper in black magic marker were three words: "Meet Holy Ghost."

Fernando stared at the three words, not comprehending.

"What do you think?" Jodie asked.

"The Foreman?" he asked.

Jodie nodded. "I don't know who else it could be. But what does it mean? Is she alive, dead, or what?"

Fernando shook his head. "You certainly seem calm, given the circumstance."

Jodie stared at him. "You should know from our work at Three Hills Ranch that I don't get hysterical. I get even."

"I remember," he said.

"So can you come with me to the house?" Jodie asked. "I want to show you the scene–get your feedback."

"Of course. I'll follow you."

"No, you can ride with me, it'll be faster," Jodie said, taking charge as she usually did. She stood and turned to go before pausing a moment. Then she turned back to Fernando and said, "But here's the thing. This has to be unofficial–off record, off grid. It's personal. Understood?"

"Understood," he repeated, following Jodie out of the office. He locked the door and climbed into her cruiser.

Jodie drove without speaking, her hands gripping the steering wheel tightly. Steady on, unflappable, she seemed focused on the task at hand, not worried about what may have happened to Sharon.

They drove out Old Santa Fe Trail to the Old Las Vegas Highway. About halfway to Bobcat Bite she turned right on Nine Mile Road, an older development of houses with spacious lots built on rolling foothills covered with piñon and ponderosa pine. Spectacular views on both sides of the road.

"We live in a smallish adobe house built in the late seventies," Jodie said.

"Before the particle board and chicken wire gentrification," Fernando added. One of his pet peeves. He disapproved of faux adobe houses made of particle board. Seemed like the ultimate insult to adobe.

"Exactly. That's why we like it," Jodie said. "Small, but we have solar heating and cooling. And the landscape is unbelievable."

Fernando saw what she meant when they turned right on a gravel driveway that led up into a stand of ponderosa pine. Situated on a small knoll, Jodie's house looked out over a forested landscape. The house itself was a simple L-shaped adobe with a tin roof and solar panels on top. Looked to be about fifteen hundred square feet–small by today's bloated standards.

"Great location," Fernando said.

Jodie nodded. She parked off to the side of the house behind a small Subaru Legacy sedan that Fernando figured belonged to Sharon, Jodie's wife.

Jodie led Fernando to the front door. The wooden door had been forced open, its small top windows smashed and its jam split by a crowbar or some other device. "Let me show you," Jodie said, stepping inside.

Jodie pointed to the damage. "So he broke in here and then entered."

Fernando followed Jodie inside the cozy adobe, thinking that Dick Murphy just found himself another customer. Old Dick should just follow him around. Be a good living.

"Sharon must have heard him banging on the door and rushed in to stop him," Jodie said, pointing to an overturned table and broken lamp on the floor. "They struggled and he dragged her back to the kitchen."

Fernando followed Jodie to the kitchen, noticing an overturned kitchen chair and an area rug on the floor twisted every which way from the struggle.

"When they reached the kitchen, he forced her down in that chair and taped her hands behind her back and maybe her feet and mouth," Jodie said. She pointed to pieces of duct tape still clinging to the chair with more unused tape hanging from the kitchen table.

Fernando examined the tape.

"Then he wrote the note with the magic marker over there on the counter," Jodie said. "After that he probably dragged her out to his car and lifted her into the trunk. I don't think he'd take a chance on putting her in the back seat. She could have raised a ruckus, even kicked out one of the rear windows."

Jodie motioned back toward the front door. "There's no blood anywhere, so it doesn't look like he hurt her–or at least bloodied her." She turned to Fernando. "So what do you think?"

"Well, it looks like a kidnapping to me," Fernando said, amazed at Jodie's ability to be so clinical at such a desperate hour.

"Exactly," Jodie replied. "I just wanted your confirmation. I would expect him to call this afternoon or tomorrow wanting a ransom. I'll take you back to your office, but stay tuned. I'll let you know as soon as he calls."

Fernando nodded. "Makes sense. But I wonder...what about the note?"

Jodie stared at him. "Yeah. What about the note?"

23

Sunday morning Estelle went to early mass, as was her habit. That left Fernando free to roam around the house while waiting for Jodie to contact him. He fully expected her to call with news of the kidnapping–that the Foreman wanted a ransom for the return of Sharon. He wondered how much the Foreman would try to extort from an underpaid county sheriff? If exorbitant, how and where would Jodie get the money to pay the ransom?

Fernando hated waiting because it took him to the dark side, brooding about past mistakes and missed opportunities, all the things he should have done differently. Guilt and regret followed him around the house like the Grim Reaper, from one room to another.

About eleven he ate an early lunch and then drove down to his office, just to pass the time. He thought a change of scenery might help. It didn't. To make matters worse, his neck of Canyon Road was closed up tight on Sunday morning, deserted. Both Essentia and Ruby's gallery, The Three Cities of Spain, were dark and shuttered as he parked his Cherokee in the empty parking lot. He felt like the proverbial last man on the face of the earth.

Feeling abandoned, Fernando walked down the gravel path to his office and unlocked the door. Inside he didn't bother to change the 'Closed' sign. Instead, he sat at his desk and took out a new legal pad. He stared at the empty sheet for a few minutes and then picked up his favorite ink pen, the one he used to generate ideas. Unfortunately, the pen generated nothing but doodles this morning. Finally he jotted down 'Foreman' and 'Meet Holy Ghost.' He stared at his scribbles for a few minutes and then started doodling again. Foreman and Holy Ghost didn't exactly fit together in any way he could imagine. Something was missing.

Fernando put away the pad and leaned back in his chair thinking. In his mind he went over the various sightings of the Foreman since his reappearance in Santa Fe. Fernando started with his experience at Three Hills Ranch, when he spotted the Foreman and the man in a white T-shirt coming out of the buildings with supplies. He ended with what Antonio's brother had told him. Daniel claimed to have seen the Foreman driving down Highway 63 from Cowles and turning west on the Old Las Vegas Highway toward Antonio's cabin and Santa Fe.

Fernando didn't know much about Highway 63, just that it ran through the National Forest all the way up to Cowles. He'd fished and camped near Cowles in the early years of his marriage before his job and his duties as a father filled up his days, but that was thirty years ago. He had no idea what the area looked like these days. Lots of hiking trails and campgrounds, he assumed. Probably more than when he last visited with his fishing buddies.

To find out more Fernando booted up his laptop and googled a map of the Pecos Wilderness. The number of small towns on Highway 63 stunned him: Lower La Posada, Upper La Posada, El Macho, Tres Lagunas, Terrero, in addition to Cowles. He had no idea. Campgrounds were scattered along the highway and on the many forest roads that branched out on both sides of the highway. He examined each of the forest roads in turn. The last one caught his attention. He did a double take. Forest Road 122 ran alongside Holy Ghost Creek to the Holy Ghost Campground and then on to the tiny, unincorporated community of Holy Ghost.

Fernando's mind raced with possibilities. This could be the breakthrough he needed, the connection between the Foreman and Holy Ghost. Was the Foreman holding Sharon somewhere on Holy Ghost Creek, either in the campground or the community? If so, did he intend to ransom Sharon? Or was he trying to set a trap for them, enticing Jodie and him up to the rugged mountain terrain on Forest Road 122 so he could pick them off one at a time with his AR-14?

It made sense, the more Fernando thought about it. Even the location made sense. The Holy Ghost area might be a long way by car from bear claw man's cabin on Shaggy Peak Trail, but it was a mere stone's throw as the crow flies. Bear claw man could have come across the Foreman as he wondered through the forest with his bears. Easily within hiking range.

Fernando's imagination spun out various scenarios, most of them bad. He had no memory of Holy Ghost Creek, but finding a missing woman anywhere in the rugged Pecos Wilderness would be difficult, if not impossible. Doubly so, given the distinct possibility that the Foreman may be waiting for them somewhere in the wilderness with an assault rifle.

Fernando vaguely recalled the history of Pecos and the origin of the Holy Ghost legend. If he remembered correctly, it was called the *espiritu santo* legend and involved the murder of a Catholic priest. Before the arrival of the Spanish, the nearby Pecos Pueblo commanded the lucrative trade routes between the plains Indians and the western and southern tribes. Prosperous and powerful, the Pecos Pueblo was home to some two thousand inhabitants living in four-and-five story stone houses. All that changed when the Spanish arrived in the late sixteenth century. The Spanish ransacked the pueblo and, in an effort to forcefully convert the Puebloans to Christianity, built a massive stone mission church and convento, one of the largest mission churches in northern New Mexico.

Resentment grew among the Puebloan people, who were reduced to the status of slaves and treated as such, until they revolted in 1680, killing hundreds of settlers and priests and driving the Spanish out of New Mexico. During the revolt the Pecos mission church, like most others in the territory, was destroyed–torn down stone by stone and then burned. The priest and lay brothers living at the mission church complex at the time of the revolt were never accounted for, but legend had it that one of the religious, possibly fray Fernando de Velasco or fray Juan de Pedraza, fled into the Pecos Wilderness, where he was hunted down and murdered by the Puebloans. Soon after the priest's murder his ghost began haunting the little creek that flowed behind and around Penitente Peak. The creek and the area around it was later named Holy Ghost or in Spanish *espiritu santo*.

That was the gist of the story that he remembered. The bottom line was that there was a holy ghost haunting the area–that is, the ghost of a priest, not the Biblical Holy Ghost.

Fernando had never been to the Holy Ghost area, but he'd heard stories from as far back as high school. Visitors seeing a specter moving among the trees, sometimes wailing mournfully. He remembered the *Independent* had done a series of stories on the ghost way back in the late 1980s or early 1990s. Supposedly the priest wandered forlornly on the banks of the Holy Ghost Creek, according to witnesses in the I*ndependent* series.

Fernando had no idea if there had been recent sightings, so he googled the campground and quickly found dozens of reviews that related stories of a ghostly presence in the forest, haunting the campground and the hiking trails. One camper last year wrote that a cold feeling overcame her body and paralyzed her when she saw the ghost walking behind the restrooms. Only later, after the ghost disappeared into the trees, did the paralysis end, allowing her to run back to her tent and close the screen, still shivering from fright. Another camper said the ghost chased him for miles along the meandering creek before disappearing into the forest. And so on, one sighting of the ghost after another.

Fernando didn't believe in ghosts, nor did he disbelieve in ghosts.

All he knew was that he'd seen something at Chaco Canyon last year while investigating the murder of a park ranger. No one would ever convince him otherwise. It made sense that if ghosts did exist, they would likely be present in New Mexico, an ancient land of 1200-year-old stone cities layered with Native American, Hispanic, and Anglo cultures. The old adage that you couldn't walk anywhere in New Mexico without walking on the bones of the Ancient Ones was literally true.

None of that made a damn bit of difference now. Fernando didn't worry about the ghost, which he would deal with if and when the time came, as he had done in Chaco Canyon. He did worry about the intentions of the Foreman, whether the Foreman had kidnapped Sharon for a ransom or was setting a trap for them at Holy Ghost. He suspected the latter.

Fernando put away his computer and called Jodie. She answered immediately.

"I know where the Foreman is hiding," Fernando said.

Silence at the other end of the line.

"That is, I think I know where he's hiding," Fernando corrected himself.

"Where?" Jodie asked finally.

"There's a campground and a small unincorporated community just off Highway Sixty-three called Holy Ghost. That's where he's hiding Sharon, I'm almost certain, either at the campground or the community."

"Never heard of it," Jodie said. "I'm from Albuquerque originally. I don't know much about these small communities."

"I mean, why else would he write 'Meet Holy Ghost'?"

"Because she's dead?" Jodie asked.

"I don't think so," Fernando said. "Did he contact you for a ransom?"

"No. I've heard nothing."

"See, I think it's a trap," Fernando said. "I think he wants to get us out in the middle of nowhere where he can ambush us. There's no better place for an ambush than Holy Ghost Creek in the Pecos Wilderness."

Jodie paused for a moment and then asked, "Is this Holy Ghost area in Santa Fe or San Miguel County?"

"San Miguel," Fernando said.

"Good. Like I said, I want this to be a private affair, off the grid," Jodie said. "Can you come right away?"

"I'm on my way," Fernando said and clicked off.

24

On his way out of town Fernando stopped at his house on Acequia Madre to pick up his Steyr. He saw Estelle's Camry parked in the garage as he pulled into their driveway, indicating Estelle was back from Sunday mass. He jumped out of the Cherokee and walked into the kitchen, where Estelle was brewing herself a cup of coffee at the counter, still dressed in her Sunday clothes. She looked at him suspiciously. "What's your hurry, it's Sunday."

"On a job," Fernando said, hurrying to the closet in his study. He removed the Steyr, still in its case, and walked back into the kitchen. He paused, suddenly feeling a surge of emotion.

Estelle stared at him.

Fernando placed the Steyr on the kitchen table. Then he went over to Estelle and gave her a hug, just in case.

Surprised, Estelle patted him on the back. "Whatever you're doing, I wish you wouldn't," she said softly.

Fernando nodded. He grabbed his Steyr and walked out of the kitchen.

Outside, he stood for a moment on their patio, shrugging off his emotion. He took a deep breath and walked to the Cherokee, placing his Steyr in the back compartment for easy access.

Then he hit the road, driving quickly around the Paseo to Old Santa Fe Trail and the Old Las Vegas Highway. The sun had already passed its zenith by the time he came to the Nine Mile Road turnoff. He swung right and entered the forested hills. When he turned into Jodie's driveway he saw her standing outside by her front door waiting for him. She wore civvies again today with an open carry shoulder holster over her black shirt. She had on heavy hiking boots.

"You're driving," Jodie said, and hopped into the Cherokee. She brought with her a bottle of water, which she placed in the cup holder between seats.

"I was just going to suggest that," Fernando said. "The roads out there are pretty rough, as I remember."

Jodie spotted the gun case in the back compartment. "I see you've brought along some firepower."

"Just in case we need it," Fernando said.

While Fernando drove back to the Old Las Vegas Highway Jodie studied a map of New Mexico. "Good God, Holy Ghost's a long way up the mountain. That's almost to Lake and Penitente peaks. The ski basin!"

Fernando laughed. "You asked for off grid."

They drove past the road to Antonio's cabin and into the town of Pecos, where Fernando turned left onto Highway 63 North. The old two-lane highway was slow going, clogged with RVs and pickups towing trailers. Everyone on the road seemed to be coming from or going to a campground. The traffic disappeared immediately when Fernando turned left on Forest Road 122. It looked like everyone was headed up to Cowles, where the majority of the campsites were located, not to Holy Ghost Campground.

"Hold on tight," Fernando said, as the Cherokee bucked and bounced over the rough road. Paved long ago, the road was now a sea of potholes and broken blacktop.

The forest seemed to close in on them as they climbed up the mountain. Tall Ponderosa pines towered above them, blocking out the sun. The landscape in front of them was wild and dark, with intermittent views of Holy Ghost Creek off to the left, a black slash through the forest. The area looked deserted with only an occasional run-down shack or abandoned cabin visible from the road. They saw no hikers or people fishing on the way up. Just a dark, ominous forest.

Not a place to explore after sunset, Fernando thought. He checked his watch. Four hours of daylight remained, although the last hour would be murky this high in the mountains.

He came to a stop at the edge of a clearing and pointed to another abandoned cabin with a collapsed roof. "What do you think, should we stop and check all the structures?"

Jodie shook her head. "I don't see tire tracks or any other indication that someone's been there recently. So no, let's go on to the campground. We don't have all that much time before sunset."

Fernando nodded and put the Cherokee in gear. He proceeded slowly up the road into a narrow canyon surrounded by massive hills on either side of the road. Eventually they came to the entrance to Holy Ghost Campground, marked by a rustic log sign listing the rules of the campground. He pulled into the first campsite, next to a picnic table and fire pit. He and Jodie climbed out of the Cherokee and studied the campground. The campsites nestled in the trees on either side of the road, all of them partially hidden. Only four were occupied, marked by tents and vehicles parked in the pull-offs. The white ghost was not one of the vehicles in the campground. That didn't necessarily mean the Foreman wasn't here. He could have parked the white ghost on one of the many unmarked forest roads or for that matter traded it for a different vehicle at a car lot or dealership in Pecos or Santa Fe.

"How do you want to do this?" Fernando asked.

Jodie pointed to the opposite side of the road. "I'll check the tents on the right side, you do the left," she said, heading across the street.

Fernando left his Steyr in the Cherokee but locked the vehicle. He walked down a narrow, meandering path that connected all the campsites on the left side of the road, like beads on a string. He sidled up to the first tent, keeping his right hand on his Smith & Wesson. The two-person tent opened on the thick green forest, its back to the road. Between the tent and the road sat an old Subaru Forester, its hood bleached white by the intense New Mexico sun.

"Anybody home?" Fernando asked, announcing himself. When no one answered, he moved to the door of the tent and peered through the netting. He saw a pile of clothes and toiletries, nothing of interest. No sign of the Foreman or Sharon. He put his Smith & Wesson in its holster.

Stepping back, he suddenly heard a noise in the woods behind him. He spun around and dropped to one knee, seeing a blurry white object as he fumbled to get his Smith & Wesson out of its holster again. What he finally saw made him laugh: a scrawny white cow, munching on grass in a clearing among the tall Ponderosa pines. The cow seemed as surprised as he was. It stared at him for a moment and then ambled away, still chewing.

The burst of adrenaline made Fernando feel jumpy. He tried to calm himself. He told himself it was only a fucking cow, get over it. Ranchers all over New Mexico had permits to graze their livestock on forest and BLM land. The Pecos Wilderness was no exception.

He paused for a few seconds to collect himself and then walked down the trail to the only other tent on his side of the road–a large red and white, six-person tent next to a Toyota Jeep. On the adjoining picnic table he saw lanterns, a Coleman stove, two Styrofoam coolers, and cardboard boxes of food and other camping supplies. Looked like serious campers.

"Anybody home?" Fernando again asked, even though he saw right away no one was around, either in the tent or outside. They were away either hiking or fishing, one or the other. To make sure he walked into the forest and around the campsite looking for what, he didn't know. He found deer and bear tracks in the trees. Maybe bear claw man wasn't as crazy as he appeared. Bears did come down to the campgrounds looking for food. They were even known to rummage through tents and garbage cans and whatever gear the campers brought with them.

When he came out of the forest he saw a large group site at the far end of the campground. The group site had multiple picnic tables lined up under a large tent and a stone fire circle. Looked like it could easily accommodate thirty or so campers. It was just as empty as the other campsites.

Finding no trace of the Foreman, he walked out into the road looking for Jodie. To the west he could see distant mountain peaks over the trees, dwarfing the campground. To the east the much lower foothills snuggled up to the campground.

Jodie waved from the last tent on her side of the road. "Nothing," she said, joining Fernando on the road.

"Same here," Fernando said.

Jodie looked at him. "What now? On to the town?"

"Actually, it's not incorporated," Fernando said. "I think it's just a group of houses."

Jodie frowned. "Oh, great, a bunch of survivalists," she said, walking off toward the Cherokee.

25

Fernando walked quickly to catch up to Jodie, feeling the effects of the high elevation. They were well over nine thousand feet above sea level here. The high altitude usually didn't bother him much unless he was hiking up a steep mountain trail. Then again, he hadn't been at this altitude for several years. Yet another sign he was getting old?

"Let's finish this," Jodie said as Fernando joined her at the Cherokee.

He glanced at her, realizing she was just as impatient as he was. They were quite a pair.

Fernando unlocked the Cherokee and climbed in behind the wheel.

Jodie hesitated. "I thought I saw something over in the trees," she said, pointing to the forest.

"It's just a cow, a white cow," Fernando said. "I saw it earlier."

"You think?" she said, climbing into the Cherokee. "Didn't look like a cow to me."

Fernando glanced at Jodie. "What do you mean?"

"Nothing," she said, turning away. She continued staring at the forest looking for something.

"Okay, then," Fernando said. He started the Cherokee and proceeded slowly up the road, which grew steeper the farther they went. The Cherokee bucked and rattled, bouncing up and down over the deep potholes. Years of ice and snow, coupled with neglect, had made the road an obstacle course. Fernando had to keep his speed between five and ten miles per hour. Dodging the bigger potholes as best as he could, he entered a long straightaway that dead-ended at a wall of round, pine-covered hills at the end of the valley. Scattered over the hills were about a dozen ramshackle structures of one kind or another. Looked like they'd all fallen from the sky and tumbled down the hillsides. He saw aging log and frame cabins, as well as sheds and outhouses constructed with rough-cut timber. One partial wooden structure looked like the opening of a mine, dug out of the hillside.

Fernando immediately pulled over on the side of the road to study the landscape. He spotted a rusted school bus that had once been painted psychedelic colors now scrapped behind one of the cabins, its hood up and its doors open. Bullet holes riddled a peace symbol on one side of the bus, as though someone had used it for target practice. There were a few other vehicles, mostly pickups, among the tumbledown buildings. The white ghost wasn't among them.

"This looks exactly how I imagined it," Jodie said.

Fernando shrugged. "Just a poor mountain community. Most of the people here work for the Forest Service. Or did, when they were working. It's probably mostly older, retired people by now."

Jodie pointed to an older woman standing in her garden on the hill closest to them. "Look. Maybe we can get some information from her."

"Exactly what I was talking about," Fernando said.

Fernando locked the Cherokee and followed Jodie up a flagstone path to the top of the hill. The woman stopped picking vegetables and watched them climb up the hill. A thin, frail looking woman with a badly humped back, she wore jeans and a gray sweatshirt, with a scarf tied around her gray hair. She put down her basket filled with ripe tomatoes and squash.

"Sorry to bother you, ma'am," Jodie said. "We're looking for a wanted man–a murderer–who we think's hiding up here. Have you seen any strangers in the houses nearby?"

The woman shook her head. "No, not in the houses. The same families have lived here for thirty, forty years, but something's been goin' on in that trailer. Ain't been no one livin' up there for years."

"Where?" Fernando asked.

The old woman pointed across the valley to the tallest hill, half again as big as the others. Just below the top was a small meadow with one of those tiny Teardrop trailers parked in front of a bulky black object, almost as big as the trailer. Fernando wondered if the black object was a woodpile covered with a tarp.

"No kidding," Fernando said. "Have you seen anyone up there?"

"No, but I sure enough heard their hollerin' and screaming last night," the woman said. "I thought somebody was getting murdered."

"That sonofabitch!" Jodie muttered. Her face had turned red with rage.

"How do you get up there?" Fernando asked. "I don't see a road."

The woman pointed to a stand of ponderosa pine down near Holy Ghost Creek. "You can't see it from here, but there's a lil' dirt road behind the trees there. That road'll take you right up to the meadow."

Fernando didn't see the road, but he saw a thin black ribbon above the meadow disappearing into a bank of aspen trees. "Is that a path or trail I see there above the meadow?"

"That's the Skyline Trail," the woman said. "It goes all the way to Lake Katherine and Santa Fe Baldy."

"No kidding. All the way to the ski basin?" Fernando asked.

The woman nodded. "You bet, but you gotta be in good shape to hike all the way to the ski basin. That's upwards of a three thousand-foot climb. There's a few backpackers who come through here ever once in a while, but not many."

Fernando noticed Jodie getting anxious to get on their way. "Okay, thanks. Much appreciated," he said.

Jodie led the way back down the hill to the Cherokee. She leaned against the hood and folded her arms across her chest. "How do you want to do this?"

"Carefully," Fernando said.

Jodie shot him a dirty look.

Fernando looked up at the trailer and considered. "Well, I guess we go up to the trailer, I don't see any other option," he said, and climbed into the Cherokee. Jodie did the same.

Fernando followed one of the many side streets branching off the main road. This one curved around the base of the hills and ended at the creek in the stand of ponderosa pine the woman had pointed out. Behind the ponderosa they found a narrow, dirt road with deep ruts climbing the hillside. From there the trailer looked to be about a quarter mile up the mountain, not far but difficult to reach because of the road. They decided to walk up the road to preserve the element of surprise.

Fernando parked alongside the creek, so that anyone seeing the Cherokee would think the driver was fishing somewhere downstream. He walked around and opened the back hatch of the Cherokee.

"Yeah, it's time to bring out the firepower," Jodie said, watching Fernando take the Steyr out of its case. She waited as he loaded the rifle and stuffed extra shells in his pockets.

"You lead the way, I'll follow," Fernando said. "This damn thing is heavy walking uphill."

Jodie nodded, leading the way up the narrow road, no wider than a hiking or animal trail. As usual, she didn't wait for Fernando. Soon she was several yards ahead of him. Occasionally she stopped to allow him to catch up, with an annoyed look on her face. He couldn't help it. The Steyr's nine pounds felt like a hundred when walking up the side of a mountain.

Stopping and starting, it took them much longer to reach the top than they expected. Jodie was running out of patience by the time they spotted the meadow up ahead, a good fifteen minutes later. The grassy meadow between them and the trailer was abloom with red, blue, and yellow wildflowers. So quiet, so pastoral that it seemed out of place, given the situation.

They left the road and entered the forest for cover. Crouching low, they approached the meadow, hiding in the thick ponderosa. Fernando took cover behind a boulder, while Jodie hid behind the trunk of a giant ponderosa with a two-foot diameter. They said nothing, trying to get a clear view of the trailer, parked about fifty yards away.

"There!" Jodie said suddenly, pointing to the trailer.

Fernando didn't like what he saw: an older Teardrop, white with black trim, with its door hanging open. Inside the door his worst fears were confirmed.

In full view, framed by the door, sat Sharon taped to a wooden chair, her head bowed. A gag of white cloth hung halfway down her chest. Her hands were taped behind the back of the chair and her ankles were taped to its legs. To complete the bondage, a length of heavy tape encircled her waist. The Foreman had set the scene perfectly, with Sharon as a decoy, the bait in the trap, an open invitation to come save the damsel in distress and get themselves blown away in the process.

Fernando studied the layout of the meadow. The black object they'd seen from the valley turned out to be a car tarp covering an automobile, partially hidden behind the trailer. He could see the front wheels of the vehicle below the tarp. The white ghost?

Fernando looked up at the mountainside, which towered over the meadow. On the mountain he saw a hiking trail snaking up through the ponderosa pines to the aspens further up the hillside. The Foreman could be hiding behind the trailer or anywhere up in the trees. It was an impossible situation for them. If they moved on the trailer, they would be sitting ducks for the Foreman's assault weapon.

After observing for a few minutes, Jodie whispered, "I'm going up to the trailer. Cover me."

Fernando reached out and grabbed her arm. "I'll go."

"No, you've got the big gun. It makes sense that you cover me," she repeated.

Fernando set up his Steyr on the boulder, sighting the trailer and then the hillside above the trailer. "Okay," he said.

Jodie sprinted out from behind the tree and ran halfway to the trailer before diving into the grass. She rolled and then raised her head slowly and glanced at the trailer. Nothing moved. No sound.

Once again Jodie jumped up and started running for the trailer.

Suddenly gunfire echoed from the hillside: Thok! Thok! Thok! One of the bullets plonked the top of the trailer, the others sliced through the meadow behind Jodie, who dove into the grass again.

Fernando trained his gun on the hillside where he'd seen flashes and fired: Crack! Crack! He had no idea whether the bullets hit anything. The flashes had come from deep in the aspen trees, about thirty or forty yards up the hill. He knew he had the advantage, because the Steyr was more accurate than an AR-14 or whatever assault weapon the Foreman was using. Not to mention that shooting downhill was always tricky, especially if you're shooting at a moving target. And Jodie was a fast-moving target.

Jodie jumped up and sprinted the last few yards to the trailer.

The Foreman fired again: Thok! Thok!

Fernando returned fire, this time with a better idea of where the shots were coming from: Crack! Crack!

Reloading, Fernando saw bushes moving on the hillside. Was the Foreman fleeing?

He watched and waited for another burst of gunfire. None came.

Jodie screamed from the trailer.

Taking his chances now, Fernando moved out from behind the boulder with the Steyr pointed up at the hillside. He didn't think the Foreman could hit him at that distance, but he for damn sure didn't want to find out. He walked slowly across the meadow, keeping an eye on the aspens he had seen moving. Then he ducked down and ran the last few yards, just in case the Foreman was trying to get a bead on him. Turned out he wasn't.

As he approached the trailer Fernando feared the worst. He had no idea what the Foreman had done to Sharon. He was relieved, sort of, when he poked his head inside the trailer and saw Jodie leaning over Sharon and trying to comfort her. Sharon gagged when Jodie pulled the white cloth out of her mouth. When she tried to talk, Sharon started coughing and shaking so hard they thought she was having a seizure. Jodie held Sharon until she stopped shaking.

Fernando felt helpless, watching Jodie work.

"Hold on, Sharon," Jodie said, cutting the tape on Sharon's hands and ankles and then the tape around her midsection.

Then Sharon slumped in the chair, nearly falling off until Fernando grabbed her and held her upright. Her eyes rolled back in her head. Fernando thought she was losing consciousness.

"It's okay, baby. You're safe now," Jodie said.

Sharon's eyes fluttered and then tried to focus. She made another attempt to speak but her voice was too hoarse to be understood. She pointed to her throat. She needed water.

"Take your time," Jodie comforted Sharon, removing the last of the tape around her midsection. "We have water in our car. We'll get you some as soon as we get you to the car."

Fernando nearly retched when he got a good look at the back of the trailer, its floor covered with garbage and rotting food tossed on the floor among roaches and mouse droppings. On the back bunk he recognized the bedding taken out of Three Hills Ranch. The thought of the Foreman sleeping on the bunk with Sharon tied to the chair further enraged Fernando.

With Jodie's help, Sharon finally managed to sit upright in the chair without falling, a thin, pale young woman with blond hair who looked as frail as Jodie was robust. Jodie wrapped her arms around Sharon and hugged her tight, trying to comfort her wife.

Fernando took the opportunity to scout around outside the trailer. The hillside seemed deserted. Maybe the Foreman had indeed fled. Maybe Fernando had wounded him with a lucky shot. He walked around behind the trailer and pulled the black tarp off the rear of the automobile. He wasn't surprised to see the white ghost. The Foreman's plan had been a good one, but even good plans can misfire. In this case it was the Steyr that had saved the day.

When he returned to the trailer he found Sharon sitting outside on the grass talking to Jodie in a gasping whisper. He saw the bruises on Sharon's face and the bloody cuts on her wrists and ankles where the tape had cut into her skin while she had been trying to free herself.

Jodie turned to Fernando angrily. "He will pay for this. I'll make damn sure of that."

Fernando nodded. "Looks like she'll be okay. At the moment we just need to get her some water." He gave himself hell for not bringing Jodie's bottle of water up the trail with them.

"Okay, let's help her to the car," Jodie said. "We'll take her to the old woman's house and leave Sharon with her while we track down the Foreman. The old woman heard the screams last night. She'll take care of Sharon until we get back. We won't give her a choice."

So Fernando and Jodie helped Sharon to her feet. Then, with Sharon in the middle and her arms around both of their shoulders, the three of them hobbled down the road to the Cherokee. Fernando had to carry the Steyr in his left hand, which made his walk even more difficult. He kept losing all the feeling in his left arm and having to pause a few minutes to regain feeling. By the time they reached the Cherokee Sharon had lost consciousness again.

Fernando drove quickly around to the old woman's house. He didn't bother to wake Sharon. Instead, he grabbed her in his arms and carried her up the sloping walkway to the old woman's house, a small cottage painted white with violet trim. A few dying flowers grew around a slab concrete porch.

Jodie went ahead and explained the situation. The old woman held open the front door and directed Fernando to carry Sharon into her living room, a small dark room with heavy curtains on the windows and throws over the sofa and chairs. Everything smelled of mold and dust.

Fernando sat Sharon on the sofa, while the old woman went to get water. She brought back a tumbler filled with water that Sharon drank quickly, spilling water on her soiled clothing.

"We'll be back," Jodie said to the old woman, who nodded.

Outside, Jodie stopped Fernando. "I'll kill the sonofabitch."

26

This time, instead of hiking, Fernando drove the Cherokee up the mountain trail to the trailer. They bounced over rocks and scraped against sage and chamisa and everything else growing on the trail. Nearing the meadow, Fernando pulled off the trail and parked in a shallow arroyo. He figured, or hoped, the Cherokee's four-wheel-drive would negotiate the sandy bottom when it came time to back out. They lumbered out of the Cherokee, Fernando carrying the heavy Steyr.

Fueled by adrenaline now, they climbed up the last twenty yards through the trees. When they reached the meadow, Jodie pointed toward the trailer and drew her weapon.

Fernando looked and saw the Foreman struggling to pull the black tarp off the white ghost. The car's windshield had been replaced since the exchange of gunfire at Joan Clark's house, Fernando noticed. Apparently the Foreman had come down from the mountain now intending to make a run for it in his Audi.

The Foreman froze when he saw Jodie. He let go of the tarp and reached for his rife. Jodie fired first, the bullet ricocheting off the top of the white ghost: Ping!

The Foreman ducked and then popped up moments later holding his AR-14.

Fernando beat him to the draw: Pop! His first shot shattered a side window of the white ghost. His second shot hit solid metal under the hood: Thunk!

Then Fernando ducked behind a Ponderosa to reload.

"Where is he?" Jodie asked.

The Foreman seemed to have disappeared by the time Fernando reloaded.

"I don't like this," Jodie said.

Fernando studied the terrain, uncertain.

"I'll circle around to the right," Jodie said. "You go to the left. Just be careful we don't shoot each other, okay?"

She eased on out to the edge of the meadow and circled to the right, always staying only a few feet away from the trees in case she needed to jump for cover. Quickly.

Fernando watched her progress, keeping an eye out for the Foreman. He figured the Steyr would be of no use in close quarters, so he hung the big gun on his back by its strap and pulled out his Smith & Wesson before leaving the protection of the trees. Then he moved out.

Fernando circled to the left, which was safer because the tree line curved around closer to the trailer on this side of the clearing. He was able to stay in the trees as he made his way behind the trailer. Coming closer, he studied the back of the trailer for a few moments but saw no sign of the Foreman. So he stepped out in the grass and walked slowly across the meadow toward the Audi, next to the trailer. The Foreman had managed to pull the tarp over the front of the vehicle, exposing the white hood and front window.

Could the Foreman be hiding inside the Audi? Seemed improbable, but the thought stopped him in mid-stride. He ducked low and circled behind the white ghost, keeping an eye on the exposed right front door. If the Foreman popped up, he would be an easy target.

He moved carefully, quietly toward the Audi. When he came close enough to touch it, he banged on the trunk with his left hand and waited.

Suddenly Jodie shouted. "Watch out! He's on the hill above us!"

Fernando spun around and dove into the grass just as the Foreman fired: Thok! Thok! Thok!

The bullets sliced through the grass, one of them grazing his left arm just above the elbow. Hurt like hell. Felt like the bullet had punctured his bicep muscle. The arm dangled at his side, useless.

Jodie fired several quick shots at the Foreman: Pop! Pop! Pop!

The Foreman stopped shooting and continued climbing up into the aspens.

"Where are you?" Jodie shouted at Fernando. "Are you okay?"

"No, I'm hit," he said, pulling a kerchief out of his rear pocket. He wrapped the cotton cloth around his bleeding bicep and pulled it tight. Then he gritted his teeth and using his right hand gently maneuvered the wounded left arm inside the strap of the Steyr to keep it from moving. Each time he moved it, the arm stung like a motherfucker. He cursed at the Foreman, who by this time had disappeared into the aspens high up on the mountain.

Jodie ran across the meadow and knelt down to examine his arm.

"I'll be okay, it's a minor wound," Fernando said, standing up. "Let's get the guy before he gets away again."

"You think?" she asked, looking skeptically at Fernando's arm.

"Let's go," Fernando said.

"Okay, you bring up the flank, I'll go on ahead," Jodie said.

Fernando watched her sprint across the meadow, admiring her athleticism. If only he were younger. He laughed out loud, remembering the old saying. If wishes were horses, even beggars would ride. Something to that effect.

He followed Jodie, walking slowly so as not to move his bleeding arm. The blood was starting to seep through the kerchief, so he stopped to pull the cloth tighter around the arm.

Fernando heard Jodie running up the trail through the aspens. The trail narrowed and became steeper the higher they climbed. Looked like a bighorn sheep trail it was so narrow. Which meant they had to be as careful as bighorn sheep climbing the dangerously narrow trail. As they neared the top of a rocky escarpment, he looked to his right over the precipice. What he saw surprised him: a two to three hundred foot drop to the bottom of a box canyon. He moved away from the cliff, steadying himself so as not to fall. He understood why this was called the Skyline Trail.

Far ahead Fernando saw Jodie standing at the rocky peak, looking down the other side of the escarpment. She had her weapon in hand.

Suddenly the Foreman came into view. He climbed up from a ledge under the lip of the cliff where he had been hiding. Struggling with his AR-14, he scrambled to his feet and pointed the assault rifle at Jodie's back. He didn't see Fernando coming up the trail quietly behind him.

"Freeze!" the Foreman shouted at Jodie.

Jodie turned around to face the Foreman.

Fernando tried to aim his Smith & Wesson at the Foreman, but his hand was shaking badly. "Drop the gun! Now!" Fernando shouted.

The Foreman spun around to face Fernando, who was still a good thirty yards away. Fernando must not have looked like an immediate threat, because the Foreman turned his attention back to Jodie. A split second too late.

Pop! Pop! Jodie's bullets struck the Foreman in the middle of his chest.

The Foreman staggered. He struggled to raise his heavy rifle.

Pop! Jodie shot him again, this time in the head.

The Foreman lost his balance and fell backwards, plunging over the edge of the precipice in a shower of loose stones.

Fernando watched the big man fall, landing with a thump at the bottom of the box canyon. The assault weapon clanged on the rock beside him.

Jodie eased over to the edge of the cliff to take a look. She tucked her Glock in its holster and smiled when she saw the Foreman wasn't moving.

How could he? He'd just taken two bullets in the chest and another in the head and fallen a couple hundred feet into the canyon.

Fernando joined her at the top. "He won't be killing any more cops."

Jodie nodded, still looking down at the twisted body of the Foreman. "Just let him lay there. Let the buzzards have him. A hiker will discover his bones in a year or two and no one will ever know who he was. Or care."

"You're a hell of a shot," Fernando said.

Jodie smiled. "Yes, I am. Now let's get you and Sharon to the Christus Saint Vincent Emergency Room. Here, give me the rifle."

She took the rifle from Fernando and put it on her back.

"Thanks," he said.

Jodie stared at him. "Can you make it down the mountain?"

Fernando glanced over the cliff at what remained of the Foreman. "Yeah, but I'll take the long way down, thank you."

27

A week later Fernando still wore his sling. A medical arm sling with Split Strap Technology and Ergonomic Design, no less. The docs had sent him home with the damn thing one day after surgery on his bicep at Christus Saint Vincent. The orthopedic surgeon said Fernando was taking an inordinate amount of time to heal, which he attributed to old age. That pissed him off big time. He'd always been a slow healer, which he attributed to a lifetime of being punched, kicked, knifed, shot, and otherwise abused physically.

Sharon had fared much better. Only cuts and abrasions from being manhandled by the Foreman. Sharon and Jodie wouldn't tell him everything the Foreman had done to Sharon, but he had his suspicions. Anyway, Sharon was examined top to bottom, in and out, and then released later that day to Jodie's care. He hadn't seen either one of them since, although he heard through the grapevine that Jodie had taken some time off to care for Sharon.

Never one to take it easy, Fernando finally acquiesced to Estelle's demand that he stay home and rest in the mornings and only go to his office for a couple of hours in the afternoon, if he absolutely had to. Which he absolutely did. He would go bonkers if he had to stay home all day puttering around the house, looking for something to do. Plus he would miss the camaraderie of the Canyon Road crowd, not to mention happy hour at El Farol.

So today, as per Estelle's instructions, he walked into his office about one o'clock. He found the light on his answering machine blinking on and off, so he sat at his desk and punched the button. Silence, then someone breathing on the other line. Then a clicking sound as whoever was breathing hung up. What the hell? Was someone trying to threaten him, intimidate him? Or was it a potential client who changed his mind in mid-call?

While he pondered this latest insult, he heard a car pull into the parking lot out front. The car must have been going too fast because he heard it spew gravel all over his Private Eye sign, which still hadn't been repaired. Followed by laughter, male laughter. He recognized the familiar voices as the two miscreants came walking down the path joking. He saw the two shadows outside his door. The big one pounded on the door, while the little one yelled, "Open up, Police!"

"No thanks," Fernando shouted.

That provoked laughter from outside. Then the door swung open and Manny walked in with a sheepish grin on his face. "Fernando, look who I brought with me," Manny said.

Behind Manny walked Antonio, all six foot, seven inches of him. The big man wore chinos and a tight blue T-shirt that revealed his bulging muscles. The only evidence of his recent hospitalization was that he seemed to have lost a few pounds. He no longer used the cane that Fernando had seen him with earlier.

"Hey, Antonio, you look great," Fernando said.

"Yeah, better than you do, at the moment," Antonio said, looking at Fernando's sling.

Fernando nodded. "I'm getting the damn thing off tomorrow. I hope. Doc says I'm not healing as fast as I should 'cause I'm old."

"Well, he got that diagnosis right, anyway," Manny joked.

Antonio smiled.

Manny laughed at his own joke. "I mean, Jesus, just look at the three of us. We look like a Wounded Warriors therapy session. I don't know about you guys, but I'm damn tired of getting used for target practice. I said I was going to quit after the Sinaloa boys put me in the hospital with a bullet through my kidney. Then the Chief talked me into coming back. What was I thinking?"

"I can relate to that," Antonio said. "I had enough of this shit in Iraq. Including two years as an MP. Tell you what, it's harder keeping the peace here because you have to read everyone their rights every time you look at them. Over there, nobody gave a damn about your rights, so piss off. So yeah, maybe I'll just say the hell with it and walk away. The Chief wouldn't try to talk me into staying. Hah! He'd be glad to get rid of me!"

Fernando shrugged. "I don't know. Estelle's still trying to get me to retire completely. To give up my private eye business and call it quits. But if I did, what the hell would I do?"

Manny looked at Antonio. "What would we do?"

"Go fishing?" Antonio asked.

"I'm sorry to have to tell you two Alpha males, but I hate fishing," Manny said. "I despise fishing. I think I would rather deal with the Sinaloa Cartel than fish."

Antonio shrugged.

"See? That's what I'm saying," Fernando said. "What would we do if we quit the profession?"

Neither Manny nor Antonio responded. Instead, they took seats in the chairs facing Fernando's desk.

Fernando looked at both men. "I'm still waiting."

"So...what happened to your arm?" Antonio asked, abruptly changing the subject.

"It's nothing. I had surgery on my bicep muscle," Fernando said, without bothering to explain.

"Hmmm," Manny said, shaking his head. "Down at the station Linda heard you and Jodie and Jodie's squeeze Sharon ended up in the Christus Saint Vincent Emergency Room last Sunday. All together."

"That right?" Fernando asked.

"Jodie supposedly claimed the three of you were hiking out on the Skyline Trail when Sharon fell and injured herself. Is that right?"

Fernando frowned. "Whatever Jodie says."

Now Antonio stepped in. "Is that how you injured your bicep? You and Sharon both falling?"

Fernando didn't like where this was headed. "Why are you guys so interested? What's up?"

"Hah! You tell us what's up," Manny said. "I mean, it's quite a coincidence that no one's seen the Foreman since that day. He seems to have disappeared. Maybe he found Jesus and decided to walk the straight and narrow. Or maybe a UFO beamed him up. What do you think?"

Antonio laughed. "You want to tell us what happened?"

Fernando shook his head. "Jodie has me sworn to secrecy."

"Wait, I know, maybe you and Sharon were getting it on and Jodie went bonkers and pushed both of you off the cliff," Manny said.

"Damn, Fernando, did you steal Jodie's wife?" Antonio added, following Manny's lead.

Fernando frowned. "Nobody stole anyone's wife."

Antonio glared at Fernando. "Then tell us what happened. We're your oldest friends, remember?"

Sighing, Fernando said, "Okay, but this is off the record, you understand? Not a word."

"That won't be a problem," Manny said. "I don't think anyone else gives a shit, anyway."

"You're probably right about that," Fernando said. "Okay, here's the gist of the story. The Foreman kidnapped Sharon and was holding her in a trailer out in Holy Ghost, the unincorporated community near Cowles in the Pecos. He ambushed Jodie and I when we went to rescue Sharon.

That was his plan all along, it wasn't to kidnap Sharon for a ransom. One of his bullets went through my left bicep. Then he started running up the Skyline Trail that goes from Holy Ghost all the way to the Santa Fe Ski Basin. We caught up with him on one of the smaller peaks and Jodie shot him. Good thing she did, because I was in no condition to shoot anybody. I could barely walk at that point. My arm hurt like hell."

"So Jodie killed him?" Manny asked.

Fernando nodded.

"Jesus, she's the one who stopped Warner too…out there at Three Hills Ranch," Antonio said. "She's a hell of a cop."

"Better than we are, probably," Fernando said.

Both Manny and Antonio stared at Fernando, as if surprised at what they'd just heard.

Finally Manny asked, "So where's the Foreman?"

"Dead," Fernando said, keeping it simple.

Manny laughed. "Yeah, but what happened to him. The body!"

"That I can't say," Fernando said.

"Can't or won't?" Manny shot back.

Fernando smiled. "Both."

Antonio looked confused. "Oh, come on…."

"He's met the Holy Ghost," Fernando said. "That's all I'm going to say about it."

Manny threw up his hands, exasperated.

"Why are we wasting our time talking about this?" Fernando asked. "We could be down the street at El Farol celebrating Happy Hour."

Manny checked his watch. "It's not Happy Hour yet."

"But it will be soon enough," Fernando said and headed for the door.

Manny and Antonio got up to follow. Manny grabbed Antonio's elbow and said, "We'll get it out of him after a few drinks. We'll call it Holy Ghost Hour."

"I heard that," Fernando said, smiling now. He stepped out into the brilliant sunshine of Canyon Road.

Readers Guide

1. After Private Investigator Fernando Lopez and Santa Fe Police Sargent Antonio Blake are ambushed, Lopez suspects a former criminal they busted is targeting them. What two leads allow Lopez to identify the assailant?

2. Describe the Foreman and why he is so dangerous. Why does Lopez notify Santa Fe County Deputy Sheriff Jodie Williams immediately on learning the shooter's identity?

3. Finding the Foreman turns out to be more difficult than identifying him. The breakthrough comes when Lopez and Williams encounter a strange woodsman wearing bear fur while pursing one of their leads on a hiking trail in the Pecos Wilderness. Describe the woodsman. What do Lopez and Williams learn about the woodsman?

4. What does the woodsman tell Lopez and Williams that will eventually help them find the Foreman?

5. Soon the hunter becomes the hunted as the Foreman discovers where Lopez lives and attacks. After the shootout, what does Lopez do to protect his wife, Estelle?

6. Things come to a head when the Foreman kidnaps Williams' wife Sharon and leaves an enigmatic note behind: "Meet Holy Ghost." How do Lopez and Williams initially react to the note?

7. Meanwhile, Sargent Blake retreats to his cabin in the Pecos Wilderness to recover from a gunshot wound suffered in the Foreman's ambush. Blake's brother, who's helping him recover, happens to spot the Foreman's car driving north out of the town of Pecos into the heart of the Pecos Wilderness. How does this development help Lopez understand the

cryptic note?

8. What does the "Holy Ghost" refer to? Explain the legend of the Pecos Holy Ghost.

9. Lopez and Williams realize they are being set up. Instead of ransoming Sharon, the Foreman is using her to lure them into a trap. Despite the danger, they head for the Holy Ghost Campground and the nearby town of Holy Ghost. Where and how do they find Sharon? What happens when they approach the trailer where the Foreman is holding Sharon?

10. Lopez is wounded in the melee that follows, leaving Williams to carry the burden. How and by whom is the Foreman finally stopped?

www.ingramcontent.com/pod-product-compliance
Lightning Source LLC
Chambersburg PA
CBHW010357310726
48979CB00006B/1072
9781632936929